THE STORY OF A PLAY

A Novel

W. D. HOWELLS

1st WORLD
LIBRARY
Literary Society

The Story of a Play

W. D. Howells

© 1st World Library, 2007
PO Box 2211
Fairfield, IA 52556
www.1stworldlibrary.com
First Edition

LCCN: 2007927866

Softcover ISBN: 978-1-4218-4581-4
Hardcover ISBN: 978-1-4218-4497-8
eBook ISBN: 978-1-4218-4665-1

Purchase *"The Story of a Play"*
as a traditional bound book at:
www.1stWorldLibrary.com/purchase.asp?ISBN=978-1-4218-4581-4

1st World Library is a literary, educational organization
dedicated to:

- Creating a free internet library of downloadable ebooks

- Hosting writing competitions and offering book publishing
scholarships.

1st World Library Literary Society

Giving Back to the World

"If you want to work on the core problem, it's early school literacy."

- James Barksdale, former CEO of Netscape

"No skill is more crucial to the future of a child, or to a democratic and prosperous society, than literacy."

- Los Angeles Times

"Literacy... means far more than learning how to read and write... The aim is to transmit... knowledge and promote social participation."

- UNESCO

"Literacy is not a luxury, it is a right and a responsibility. If our world is to meet the challenges of the twenty-first century we must harness the energy and creativity of all our citizens."

- President Bill Clinton

"Parents should be encouraged to read to their children, and teachers should be equipped with all available techniques for teaching literacy, so the varying needs and capacities of individual kids can be taken into account."

- Hugh Mackay

I

The young actor who thought he saw his part in Maxwell's play had so far made his way upward on the Pacific Coast that he felt justified in taking the road with a combination of his own. He met the author at a dinner of the Papyrus Club in Boston, where they were introduced with a facile flourish of praise from the journalist who brought them together, as the very men who were looking for each other, and who ought to be able to give the American public a real American drama. The actor, who believed he had an ideal of this drama, professed an immediate interest in the kind of thing Maxwell told him he was trying to do, and asked him to come the next day, if he did not mind its being Sunday, and talk the play over with him.

He was at breakfast when Maxwell came, at about the hour people were getting home from church, and he asked the author to join him. But Maxwell had already breakfasted, and he hid his impatience of the actor's politeness as well as he could, and began at the first moment possible: "The idea of my play is biblical; we're still a very biblical people." He had thought of the fact in seeing so many worshippers swarming out of the churches.

"That is true," said the actor.

"It's the old idea of the wages of sin. I should like to call it that."

"The name has been used, hasn't it?"

"I shouldn't mind; for I want to get a new effect from the old notion, and it would be all the stronger from familiar association with the name. I want to show that the wages of sin is more sinning, which is the very body of death."

"Well?"

"Well, I take a successful man at the acme of his success, and study him in a succession of scenes that bring out the fact of his prosperity in a way to strike the imagination of the audience, even the groundlings; and, of course, I have to deal with success of the most appreciable sort—a material success that is gross and palpable. I have to use a large canvas, as big as Shakespeare's, in fact, and I put in a great many figures."

"That's right," said the actor. "You want to keep the stage full, with people coming and going."

"There's a lot of coming and going, and a lot of incidents, to keep the spectator interested, and on the lookout for what's to happen next. The whole of the first act is working up to something that I've wanted to see put on the stage for a good while, or ever since I've thought of writing for the stage, and that is a large dinner, one of the public kind."

"Capital!" said the actor.

"I've seen a good deal of that sort of thing as a reporter; you know they put us at a table off to one side, and we see the whole thing, a great deal better than the diners themselves

W. D. Howells

do. It's a banquet, given by a certain number of my man's friends, in honor of his fiftieth birthday, and you see the men gathering in the hotel parlor—well, you can imagine it in almost any hotel—and Haxard is in the foreground. Haxard is the hero's name, you know."

"It's a good name," the actor mused aloud. "It has a strong sound."

"Do you like it? Well, Haxard," Maxwell continued, "is there in the foreground, from the first moment the curtain rises, receiving his friends, and shaking hands right and left, and joking and laughing with everybody—a very small joke makes a very large laugh on occasions like that, and I shall try to give some notion of the comparative size of the joke and the laugh—and receiving congratulations, that give a notion of what the dinner is for, and the kind of man he is, and how universally respected and all that, till everybody has come; and then the doors between the parlor and the dining-room are rolled back, and every man goes out with his own wife, or his sister, or his cousin, or his aunt, if he hasn't got a wife; I saw them do that once, at a big commercial dinner I reported."

"Ah, I was afraid it was to be exclusively a man's dinner!" the actor interrupted.

"Oh, no," Maxwell answered, with a shade of vexation. "That wouldn't do. You couldn't have a scene, or, at least, not a whole act, without women. Of course I understand that. Even if you could keep the attention of the audience without them, through the importance of the intrigue, still you would have to have them for the sake of the stage-picture. The drama is literature that makes a double appeal; it appeals to the sense as well as the intellect, and the stage is half the time merely a picture-frame. I had to think that out pretty early."

The actor nodded. "You couldn't too soon."

"It wouldn't do to have nothing but a crowd of black coats and white shirt-fronts on the stage through a whole act. You want color, and a lot of it, and you can only get it, in our day, with the women's costumes. Besides, they give movement and life. After the dinner begins they're supposed to sparkle all through. I've imagined the table set down the depth of the stage, with Haxard and the nominal host at the head, fronting the audience, and the people talking back and forth on each side, and I let the ladies do most of the talking, of course. I mean to have the dinner served through all the courses, and the waiters coming and going; the events will have to be hurried, and the eating merely sketched, at times; but I should keep the thing in pretty perfect form, till it came to the speaking. I shall have to cut that a good deal, but I think I can give a pretty fair notion of how they butter the object of their hospitality on such occasions; I've seen it and heard it done often enough. I think, perhaps, I shall have the dinner an act by itself. There are only four acts in the play now, and I'll have to make five. I want to give Haxard's speech as fully as possible, for that's what I study the man in, and make my confidences to the audience about him. I shall make him butter himself, but all with the utmost humility, and brag of everything that he disclaims the merit of."

The actor rose and reached across the table for the sugar. "That's a capital notion. That's new. That would make a hit— the speech would."

"Do you think so?" returned the author. "*I* thought so. I believe that in the hands of a good actor the speech could be made tremendously telling. I wouldn't have a word to give away his character, his nature, except the words of his own

W. D. Howells

mouth, but I would have them do it so effectually that when he gets through the audience will be fairly 'onto him,' don't you know."

"Magnificent!" said the actor, pouring himself some more cocoa.

Maxwell continued: "In the third act—for I see that I shall have to make it the third now—the scene will be in Haxard's library, after he gets home from the complimentary dinner, at midnight, and he finds a man waiting for him there—a man that the butler tells him has called several times, and was so anxious to see him that Mrs. Haxard has given orders to let him wait. Oh, I ought to go back a little, and explain—"

"Yes, do!" The actor stirred his cocoa with mounting interest. "Yes, don't leave anything out."

"I merely meant to say that in the talk in the scene, or the act, before the dinner—I shall have two acts, but with no wait between them; just let down the curtain and raise it again—it will come out that Haxard is not a Bostonian by birth, but has come here since the war from the Southwest, where he went, from Maine, to grow up with the country, and is understood to have been a sort of quiescent Union man there; it's thought to be rather a fine thing the way he's taken on Boston, and shown so much local patriotism and public spirit and philanthropy, in the way he's brought himself forward here. People don't know a great deal about his past, but it's understood to have been very creditable. I shall have to recast that part a little, and lengthen the delay before he comes on, and let the guests, or the hosts—for *they're* giving *him* the dinner—have time to talk about him, and free their minds in honor of him behind his back, before they begin to his face."

"Never bring your principal character on at once," the actor interjected.

"No," Maxwell consented. "I see that wouldn't have done." He went on: "Well, as soon as Haxard turns up the light in his library, the man rises from the lounge where he has been sitting, and Haxard sees who it is. He sees that it is a man whom he used to be in partnership with in Texas, where they were engaged in some very shady transactions. They get caught in one of them—I haven't decided yet just what sort of transaction it was, and I shall have to look that point up; I'll get some law-student to help me—and Haxard, who wasn't Haxard then, pulls out and leaves his partner to suffer the penalty. Haxard comes North, and after trying it in various places, he settles here, and marries, and starts in business and prospers on, while the other fellow takes their joint punishment in the penitentiary. By the way, it just occurs to me! I think I'll have it that Haxard has killed a man, a man whom he has injured; he doesn't mean to kill him, but he has to; and this fellow is knowing to the homicide, but has been prevented from getting onto Haxard's trail by the consequences of his own misdemeanors; that will probably be the best way out. Of course it all has to transpire, all these facts, in the course of the dialogue which the two men have with each other in Haxard's library, after a good deal of fighting away from the inevitable identification on Haxard's part. After the first few preliminary words with the butler at the door before he goes in to find the other man—his name is Greenshaw—"

"That's a good name, too," said the actor.

"Yes, isn't it? It has a sort of probable sound, and yet it's a made-up name. Well, I was going to say—"

"And I'm glad you have it a homicide that Haxard is guilty

W. D. Howells

of, instead of a business crime of some sort. That sort of crime never tells with an audience," the actor observed.

"No," said Maxwell. "Homicide is decidedly better. It's more melodramatic, and I don't like that, but it will be more appreciable, as a real sin, to most of the audience; we steal and cheat so much, and we kill comparatively so little in the North. Well, I was going to say that I shall have this whole act to consist entirely of the passage between the two men. I shall let it begin with a kind of shiver creeping over the spectator, when he recognizes the relation between them, and I hope I shall be able to make it end with a shudder, for Haxard must see from the first moment, and he must let the audience see at last, that the only way for him to save himself from his old crime is to commit a new one. He must kill the man who saw him kill a man."

"That's good," the actor thoughtfully murmured, as if tasting a pleasant morsel to try its flavor. "Excellent."

Maxwell laughed for pleasure, and went on: "He arranges to meet the man again at a certain time and place, and that is the last of Greenshaw. He leaves the house alone; and the body of an unknown man is found floating up and down with the tide under the Long Bridge. There are no marks of violence; he must have fallen off the bridge in the dark, and been drowned; it could very easily happen. Well, then comes the most difficult part of the whole thing; I have got to connect the casualty with Haxard in the most unmistakable way, unmistakable to the audience, that is; and I have got to have it brought home to him in a supreme moment of his life. I don't want to have him feel remorse for it; that isn't the modern theory of the criminal; but I do want him to be anxious to hide his connection with it, and to escape the consequences. I don't know but I shall try another dinner-scene, though I am afraid it would be a risk."

The actor said, "I don't know. It might be the very thing. The audience likes a recurrence to a distinctive feature. It's like going back to an effective strain in music."

"Yes," Maxwell resumed, "slightly varied. I might have a private dinner this time; perhaps a dinner that Haxard himself is giving. Towards the end the talk might turn on the case of the unknown man, and the guests might discuss it philosophically together; Haxard would combat the notion of a murder, and even of a suicide; he would contend for an accident, pure and simple. All the fellows would take a turn at the theory, but the summing-up opinion I shall leave to a legal mind, perhaps the man who had made the great complimentary speech at the public dinner to Haxard in the first act. I should have him warm to his work, and lay it down to Haxard in good round fashion, against his theory of accident. He could prove to the satisfaction of everybody that the man who was last seen with the drowned man—or was supposed to have been seen with him—according to some very sketchy evidence at the inquest, which never amounted to anything—was the man who pushed him off the bridge. He could gradually work up his case, and end the argument with a semi-jocular, semi-serious appeal to Haxard himself, like, 'Why, suppose it was your own case,' and so forth, and so forth, and so forth, and then suddenly stop at something he notices queer in Haxard, who is trying to get to his feet. The rest applaud: 'That's right! Haxard has the floor,' and so on, and then Haxard slips back into his chair, and his head falls forward—I don't like death-scenes on the stage. They're usually failures. But if this was managed simply, I think it would be effective."

The actor left the table and began to walk about the room. "I shall want that play. I can see my part in Haxard. I know just how I could make up for him. And the play is so native, so American, that it will go like wildfire."

W. D. Howells

The author heard these words with a swelling heart. He did not speak, for he could not. He sat still, watching the actor as he paced to and fro, histrionically rapt in his representation of an actor who had just taken a piece from a young dramatist. "If you can realize that part as you've sketched it to me," he said, finally, "I will play it exclusively, as Jefferson does Rip Van Winkle. There are immense capabilities in the piece. Yes, sir; that thing will run for years!"

"Of course," Maxwell found voice to say, "there is one great defect in it, from the conventional point of view." The actor stopped and looked at him. "There's no love-business."

"We must have that. But you can easily bring it in."

"By the head and shoulders, yes. But I hate love-making on the stage, almost as much as I do dying. I never see a pair of lovers beyond the footlights without wanting to kill them." The actor remained looking at him over his folded arms, and Maxwell continued, with something like a personal rancor against love-making, while he gave a little, bitter laugh, "I might have it somehow that Haxard had killed a pair of stage-lovers, and this was what Greenshaw had seen him do. But that would have been justifiable homicide."

The actor's gaze darkened into a frowning stare, as if he did not quite make out this kind of fooling. "All the world loves a lover," he said, tentatively.

"I don't believe it does," said Maxwell, "except as it's stupid, and loves anything that makes it laugh. It loves a comic lover, and in the same way it loves a droll drunkard or an amusing madman."

"We shall have to have some sort of love-business," the actor returned, with an effect of leaving the right interpretation of

Maxwell's peculiar humor for some other time. "The public wants it. No play would go without it. You can have it subordinate if you like, but you have got to have it. How old did you say Haxard was?"

"About fifty. Too old for a lover, unless you could make him in love with some one else's wife, as he has one of his own already. But that wouldn't do."

The actor looked as if he did not know why it would not do, but he said, "He could have a daughter."

"Yes, and his daughter could have a lover. I had thought of something of that kind, and of bringing in their ill-fated passion as an element of the tragedy. We could have his disgrace break their hearts, and kill two birds with one stone, and avenge a long-suffering race of playwrights upon stage-lovers."

The actor laughed like a man of small humor, mellowly, but hollowly. "No, no! We must have the love-affair end happily. You can manage that somehow. Have you got the play roughed out at all?"

"Not in manuscript. I've only got it roughed out in my mind."

"Well, I want that play. That's settled. I can't do anything with it this winter, but I should like to open with it next fall. Do you think you could have it ready by the end of July?"

II

They sat down and began to talk times and terms. They parted with a perfect understanding, and Maxwell was almost as much deceived as the actor himself. He went home full of gay hopes to begin work on the play at once, and to realize the character of Haxard with the personality of the actor in his eye. He heard nothing from him till the following spring, when the actor wrote with all the ardor of their parting moment, to say that he was coming East for the summer, and meant to settle down in the region of Boston somewhere, so that they could meet constantly and make the play what they both wanted. He said nothing to account for his long silence, and he seemed so little aware of it that Maxwell might very well have taken it for a simple fidelity to the understanding between them, too unconscious to protest itself. He answered discreetly, and said that he expected to pass the summer on the coast somewhere, but was not yet quite certain where he should be; that he had not forgotten their interview, and should still be glad to let him have the play if he fancied it. Between this time and the time when the actor appeared in person, he sent Maxwell several short notes, and two or three telegrams, sufficiently relevant but not very necessary, and when his engagement ended in the West, a fortnight after Maxwell was married, he telegraphed again and then came through without a stop from Denver, where the combination broke up, to

Manchester-by-the-Sea. He joined the little colony of actors which summers there, and began to play tennis and golf, and to fish and to sail, almost without a moment's delay. He was not very fond of any of these things, and in fact he was fond only of one thing in the world, which was the stage; but he had a theory that they were recreation, and that if he went in for them he was building himself up for the season, which began early in September; he had appropriate costumes for all of them, and no one dressed the part more perfectly in tennis or golf or sailing or fishing. He believed that he ought to read up in the summer, too, and he had the very best of the recent books, in fiction and criticism, and the new drama. He had all of the translations of Ibsen, and several of Maeterlinck's plays in French; he read a good deal in his books, and he lent them about in the hotel even more. Among the ladies there he had the repute of a very modern intellect, and of a person you would never take for an actor, from his tastes. What his tastes would have been if you had taken him for an actor, they could not have said, perhaps, but probably something vicious, and he had not a vice. He did not smoke, and he did not so much as drink tea or coffee; he had cocoa for breakfast, and at lunch a glass of milk, with water at dinner. He had a tint like the rose, and when he smiled or laughed, which was often, from a constitutional amiability and a perfect digestion, his teeth showed white and regular, and an innocent dimple punctured either cheek. His name was Godolphin, for he had instinctively felt that in choosing a name he might as well take a handsome one while he was about it, and that if he became Godolphin there was no reason why he should not become Launcelot, too. He did not put on these splendors from any foible, but from a professional sense of their value in the bills; and he was not personally characterized by them. As Launcelot Godolphin he was simpler than he would have been with a simpler name, and it was his ideal to be modest in everything that personally belonged to him. He studied an unprofessional walk, and a very colloquial tone in speaking. He was of course clean-shaven, but during the summer he let his mustache grow, though he was aware that he looked better without it. He was tall, and he carried himself with the vigor of his perfect health; but on the stage he looked less than his real size, like a perfectly proportioned edifice.

Godolphin wanted the Maxwells to come to his hotel in Manchester, but there were several reasons for their not doing this; the one Maxwell alleged was that they could not afford it. They had settled for the summer, when they got home after their brief wedding journey, at a much cheaper house in Magnolia, and the actor and the author were then only three miles apart, which Mrs. Maxwell thought was quite near enough. "As it is," she said, "I'm only afraid he'll be with you every moment with his suggestions, and won't let you have any chance to work out your own conceptions."

Godolphin had not failed to notify the public through the press that Mr. Brice Maxwell had severed his connection with the Boston *Abstract*, for the purpose of devoting himself to a new play for Mr. Launcelot Godolphin, and he thought it would have been an effective touch if it could have been truthfully reported that Mr. Godolphin and Mr. Maxwell might be seen almost any day swinging over the roads together in the neighborhood of Manchester, blind and deaf to all the passing, in their discussion of the play, which they might almost be said to be collaborating. But failing Maxwell's consent to anything of the sort, Godolphin did the swinging over the roads himself, so far as the roads lay between Manchester and Magnolia. He began by coming in the forenoon, when he broke Maxwell up fearfully, but he was retarded by a waning of his own ideal in the matter, and finally got to arriving at that hour in the afternoon when Maxwell could be found revising his morning's work, or lying at his wife's feet on the rocks, and now and then irrelevantly bringing up a knotty point in the character or action for her criticism. For these excursions Godolphin had equipped himself with a gray corduroy sack and knicker-bockers, and a stick which he cut from the alder thicket; he wore russet shoes of ample tread, and very thick-ribbed stockings, which became his stalwart calves.

Nothing could be handsomer than the whole effect he made in this costume, and his honest face was a pleasure to look at, though its intelligence was of a kind so wholly different from the intelligence of Maxwell's face, that Mrs. Maxwell always had a struggle with herself before she could allow that it was intelligence at all. He was very polite to her; he always brought her flowers, and he opened doors, and put down windows, and leaped to his feet for every imaginable occasion of hers, in a way that Maxwell never did, and somehow a way that the polite men of her world did not, either. She had to school herself to believe him a gentleman, and she would not accept a certain vivid cleanliness he had as at all aristocratic; she said it was too fresh, and he ought to have carried a warning placard of "Paint." She found that Godolphin had one great and constant merit: he believed in Maxwell's genius as devoutly as she did herself. This did not prevent him from coming every day with proposals for changes in the play, more or less structural. At one time he wished the action laid in some other country and epoch, so as to bring in more costume and give the carpenter something to do; he feared that the severity of the *mise en scene* would ruin the piece. At another time he wanted lines taken out of the speeches of the inferior characters and put into his own, to fatten the part, as he explained. At other times he wished to have paraphrases of passages that he had brought down the house with in other plays written into this; or scenes transposed, so that he would make a more effective entrance here or there. There was no end to his inventions for spoiling the simplicity and truthfulness of Maxwell's piece, which he

W. D. Howells

yet respected for the virtues in it, and hoped the greatest things from.

One afternoon he arrived with a scheme for a very up-to-date scene in the last act; have it a supper instead of a dinner, and then have a skirt-dancer introduced, as society people had been having Carmencita. "When Haxard dies, you know," he explained, "it would be tremendously effective to have the woman catch him in her arms, and she would be a splendid piece of color in the picture, with Haxard's head lying in her lap, as the curtain comes down with a run."

At this suggestion Mrs. Maxwell was too indignant to speak; her husband merely said, with his cold smile, "Yes; but I don't see what it would have to do with the rest of the play."

"You could have it," said Godolphin, "that he was married to a Mexican during his Texas episode, and this girl was their daughter." Maxwell still smiled, and Godolphin deferred to his wife: "But perhaps Mrs. Maxwell would object to the skirt-dance?"

"Oh, no," she answered, ironically, "I shouldn't mind having it, with Carmencita in society for a precedent. But," she added, "the incident seems so out of keeping with the action and the temperament of the play, and everything. If I were to see such a thing on the stage, merely as an impartial spectator, I should feel insulted."

Godolphin flushed. "I don't see where the insult would come in. You mightn't like it, but it would be like anything else in a play that you were not personally concerned in."

"No, excuse me, Mr. Godolphin. I think the audience is as much concerned in the play as the actor or the author, and if either of these fails in the ideal, or does a bit of clap-trap when they have wrought the audience up in expectation of something noble, then they insult the audience—or all the better part of it."

"The better part of the audience never fills the house," said the actor.

"Very well. I hope my husband will never write for the worse part."

"And I hope I shall never play to it," Godolphin returned, and he looked hurt at the insinuation of her words.

"It isn't a question of all that," Maxwell interposed, with a worried glance at his wife. "Mr. Godolphin has merely suggested something that can be taken into the general account; we needn't decide it now. By the way," he said to the actor, "have you thought over that point about changing Haxard's crime, or the quality of it? I think it had better not be an intentional murder; that would kill the audience's sympathy with him from the start, don't you think? We had better have it what they call a rencontre down there, where two gentlemen propose to kill each other on sight. Greenshaw's hold on him would be that he was the only witness of the fight, and that he could testify to a wilful murder if he chose. Haxard's real crime must be the killing of Greenshaw."

"Yes," said Godolphin, and he entered into the discussion of the effect this point would have with the play. Mrs. Maxwell was too much vexed to forgive him for making the suggestion which he had already dropped, and she left the room for fear she should not be able to govern herself at the sight of her husband condescending to temporize with him. She thought that Maxwell's willingness to temporize, even when it involved no insincerity, was a defect in his character;

W. D. Howells

she had always thought that, and it was one of the things that she meant to guard him against with all the strength of her zeal for his better self. When Godolphin was gone at last, she lost no time in coming back to Maxwell, where he sat with the manuscript of his play before him, apparently lost in some tangle of it. She told him abruptly that she did not understand how, if he respected himself, if he respected his own genius, he could consider such an idea as Godolphin's skirt-dance for an instant.

"Did I consider it?" he asked.

"You made him think so."

"Well," returned Maxwell, and at her reproachful look he added, "Godolphin never thought I was considering it. He has too much sense, and he would be astonished and disgusted if I took him in earnest and did what he wanted. A lot of actors get round him over there, and they fill him up with all sorts of stage notions, and what he wants of me is that I shall empty him of them and yet not put him to shame about them. But if you keep on in that way you took with him he'll throw me over."

"Well, let him!" cried Mrs. Maxwell. "There are twenty other actors who would jump at the chance to get such a play."

"Don't you believe it, my dear. Actors don't jump at plays, and Godolphin is the one man for me. He's young, and has the friendly regard from the public that a young artist has, and yet he isn't identified with any part in particular, and he will throw all his force into creating this, as he calls it."

"I can't bear to have him use that word, Brice. *You* created it."

"The word doesn't matter. It's merely a technical phrase. I shouldn't know where to turn if he gave it up."

"Pshaw! You could go to a manager."

"Thank you; I prefer an actor. Now, Louise, you must not be so abrupt with Godolphin when he comes out with those things."

"I can't help it, dearest. They are insulting to you, and insulting to common-sense. It's a kindness to let him know how they would strike the public. I don't pretend to be more than the average public."

"He doesn't feel it a kindness the way you put it."

"Then you don't like me to be sincere with him! Perhaps you don't like me to be sincere with *you* about your play?"

"Be as sincere with me as you like. But this—this is a matter of business, and I'd rather you wouldn't."

"Rather I wouldn't say anything at all?" demanded Louise.

"I didn't say so, and you know I didn't; but if you can't get on without ruffling Godolphin, why, perhaps—"

"Very well, then, I'll leave the room the next time he comes. That will be perfectly simple; and it will be perfectly simple to do as most other people would—not concern myself with the play in any way from this out. I dare say you would prefer that, too, though I didn't quite expect it to come to that before our honeymoon was out."

"Oh, now, my dear!"

W. D. Howells

"You know it's so. But I can do it! I might have expected it from a man who was so perfectly self-centred and absorbed. But I was such a fool—" Her tears came and her words stopped.

Maxwell leaned forward with his thin face between his hands. This made him miserable, personally, but he was not so miserable but his artistic consciousness could take note of the situation as a very good one, and one that might be used effectively on the stage. He analyzed it perfectly in that unhappy moment. She was jealous of his work, which she had tolerated only while she could share it, and if she could not share it, while some other was suffered to do so, it would be cruel for her. But he knew that he could not offer any open concession now without making bad worse, and he must wait till the right time for it came. He had so far divined her, without formulating her, that he knew she would be humiliated by anything immediate or explicit, but would later accept a tacit repentance from him; and he instinctively forebore.

III

For the present in her resentment of his willingness to abase his genius before Godolphin, or even to hold it in abeyance, Mrs. Maxwell would not walk to supper with her husband in the usual way, touching his shoulder with hers from time to time, and making herself seem a little lower in stature by taking the downward slope of the path leading from their cottage to the hotel. But the necessity of appearing before the people at their table on as perfect terms with him as ever had the effect that conduct often has on feeling, and she took his arm in going back to their cottage, and leaned tenderly upon him.

Their cottage was one of the farthest from the hotel, and the smallest and quietest. In fact there was yet no one in it but themselves, and they dwelt there in an image of home, with the sole use of the veranda and the parlor, where Maxwell had his manuscripts spread about on the table as if he owned the place. A chambermaid came over from the hotel in the morning to put the cottage in order, and then they could be quite alone there for the rest of the day.

"Shall I light the lamp for you, Brice?" his wife asked, as they mounted the veranda steps.

"No," he said, "let us sit out here," and they took the

W. D. Howells

arm-chairs that stood on the porch, and swung to and fro in silence for a little while. The sea came and went among the rocks below, marking its course in the deepening twilight with a white rope of foam, and raving huskily to itself, with now and then the long plunge of some heavier surge against the bowlders, and a hoarse shout. The Portland boat swam by in the offing, a glitter of irregular lights, and the lamps on the different points of the Cape blinked as they revolved in their towers. "This is the kind of thing you can get only in a novel," said Maxwell, musingly. "You couldn't possibly give the feeling of it in a play."

"Couldn't you give the feeling of the people looking at it?" suggested his wife, and she put out her hand to lay it on his.

"Yes, you could do that," he assented, with pleasure in her notion; "and that would be better. I suppose that is what would be aimed at in a description of the scene, which would be tiresome if it didn't give the feeling of the spectator."

"And Godolphin would say that if you let the carpenter have something to do he would give the scene itself, and you could have the effect of it at first hand."

Maxwell laughed. "I wonder how much they believe in those contrivances of the carpenter themselves. They have really so little to do with the dramatic intention; but they have been multiplied so since the stage began to make the plays that the actors are always wanting them in. I believe the time will come when the dramatist will avoid the occasion or the pretext for them."

"That will be after Godolphin's time," said Mrs. Maxwell.

"Well, I don't know," returned Maxwell. "If Godolphin should happen to imagine doing without them he would go all lengths."

"Or if you imagined it and let him suppose he had. He never imagines anything of himself."

"No, he doesn't. And yet how perfectly he grasps the notion of the thing when it is done! It is very different from literature, acting is. And yet literature is only the representation of life."

"Well, acting is the representation of life at second-hand, then, and it ought to be willing to subordinate itself. What I can't bear in Godolphin is his setting himself up to be your artistic equal. He is no more an artist than the canvas is that the artist paints a picture on."

Maxwell laughed. "Don't tell him so; he won't like it."

"I will tell him so some day, whether he likes it or not."

"No, you mustn't; for it isn't true. He's just as much an artist in his way as I am in mine, and, so far as the public is concerned, he has given more proofs."

"Oh, *his* public!"

"It won't do to despise any public, even the theatre-going public." Maxwell added the last words with a faint sigh.

"It's always second-rate," said his wife, passionately. "Third-rate, fourth-rate! Godolphin was quite right about that. I wish you were writing a novel, Brice, instead of a play. Then you would be really addressing refined people."

"It kills me to have you say that, Louise."

"Well, I won't. But don't you see, then, that you must stand up for art all the more unflinchingly if you intend to write plays that will refine the theatre-going public, or create a new one? That is why I can't endure to have you even seem to give way to Godolphin."

"You must stand it so long as I only seem to do it. He's far more manageable than I expected him to be. It's quite pathetic how docile he is, how perfectly ductile! But it won't do to browbeat him when he comes over here a little out of shape. He's a curious creature," Maxwell went on with a relish in Godolphin, as material, which his wife suffered with difficulty. "I wonder if he could ever be got into a play. If he could he would like nothing better than to play himself, and he would do it to perfection; only it would be a comic part, and Godolphin's mind is for the serious drama." Maxwell laughed. "All his artistic instincts are in solution, and it needs something like a chemical agent to precipitate them, or to give them any positive character. He's like a woman!"

"Thank you," said Mrs. Maxwell.

"Oh, I mean all sorts of good things by that. He has the sensitiveness of a woman."

"Is that a good thing? Then I suppose he was so piqued by what I said about his skirt-dance that he will renounce you."

"Oh, I don't believe he will. I managed to smooth him up after you went out."

Mrs. Maxwell sighed. "Yes, you are very patient, and if you are patient, you are good. You are better than I am."

"I don't see the sequence exactly," said Maxwell.

They were both silent, and she seemed to have followed his devious thought in the same muse, for when he spoke again she did not reproach him with an equal inconsequence. "I don't know whether I could write a novel, and, besides, I think the drama is the supreme literary form. It stands on its own feet. It doesn't have to be pushed along, or pulled along, as the novel does."

"Yes, of course, it's grand. That's the reason I can't bear to have you do anything unworthy of it."

"I know, Louise," he said, tenderly, and then again they did not speak for a little while.

He emerged from their silence, at a point apparently very remote, with a sigh. "If I could only know just what the feelings of a murderer really were for five minutes, I could out-Shakespeare Shakespeare in that play. But I shall have to trust to the fall of man, and the general depravity of human nature, I suppose. After all, there's the potentiality of every kind of man in every man. If you've known what it is to hate, you've known what it is to kill."

"I felt once as if I had killed *you*," she said, and then he knew that she was thinking of a phase of their love which had a perpetual fascination for them both. "But I never hated you."

"No; I did the hating," he returned, lightly.

"Ah, don't say so, dear," she entreated, half in earnest.

"Well, have it all to yourself, then," he said; and he rose and went indoors, and lighted the lamp, and she saw him get out the manuscript of his play, while she sat still, recalling the time when she had tried to dismiss him from her thoughts upon a theory of his unworthiness. He had not yet spoken of love to her then, but she felt as if she had refused to listen to him, and her remorse kept his image before her in an attitude of pathetic entreaty for at least a hearing. She knew that she had given him reason, if she had not given him courage, to believe that she cared for him; but he was too proud to renew the tacit approaches from which she had so abruptly retreated, and she had to invite them from him.

When she began to do this with the arts so imperceptible to the single-mindedness of a man, she was not yet sure whether she could endure to live with him or not; she was merely sure that she could not live without him, or, to be more specific, without his genius, which she believed no one else appreciated as she did. She believed that she understood his character better than any one else, and would know how to supplement it with her own. She had no ambition herself, but she could lend him a more telescopic vision in his, and keep his aims high, if his self-concentration ever made him short-sighted. He would write plays because he could not help it, but she would inspire him to write them with the lofty sense of duty she would have felt in writing them if she had his gifts.

She was as happy in their engagement and as unhappy as girls usually are during their courtship. It is the convention to regard those days as very joyous, but probably no woman who was honest about the fact would say that they were so from her own experience. Louise found them full of excitement and an interest from which she relaxed at times with such a sense of having strained forward to their end that she had a cold reluctance from Maxwell, and though she never dreamed of giving him up again, she sometimes wished she had never seen him. She was eager to have it all over, and be married and out of the way, for one thing because she knew that Maxwell could never be assimilated to her circumstance, and she should have no rest till she was assimilated to his. When it came to the dinners and lunches, which the Hilary kinship and friendship made in honor of her engagement, she found that Maxwell actually thought she could make excuse of his work to go without him, and she had to be painfully explicit before she could persuade him that this would not do at all. He was not timid about meeting her friends, as he might very well have been; but, in comparison with his work, he apparently held them of little moment, and at last he yielded to her wishes rather than her reasons. He made no pretence of liking those people, but he gave them no more offence than might have been expected. Among the Hilary cousins there were several clever women, who enjoyed the quality of Maxwell's somewhat cold, sarcastic humor, and there were several men who recognized his ability, though none of them liked him any better than he liked them. He had a way of regarding them all at first as of no interest, and then, if something kindled his imagination from them, of showing a sudden technical curiosity, which made the ladies, at least, feel as if he were dealing with them as so much material. They professed to think that it was only a question of time when they should all reappear in dramatic form, unless Louise should detect them in the manuscript before they were put upon the stage and forbid his using them. If it were to be done before marriage they were not sure that she would do it, or could do it, for it was plain to be seen that she was perfectly infatuated with him. The faults they found in him were those of manner mostly, and they perceived that these were such as passion might forgive to his other qualities. There were some who said that they envied her for being so much in love with him, but these were not many; and some did not find him good-looking, or see what could have taken her with him.

Maxwell showed himself ignorant of the observances in every way, and if Louise had not rather loved him the more for what he made her suffer because of them, she must

W. D. Howells

certainly have given him up at times. He had never, to her thinking, known how to put a note properly on paper; his letters were perfectly fascinating, but they lacked a final charm in being often written on one side of half-sheets, and numbered in the upper right-hand corner, like printer's copy. She had to tell him that he must bring his mother to call upon her; and then he was so long doing it that Louise imagined a timidity in his mother which he was too proud to own, and made her own mother go with her to see Mrs. Maxwell in the house which she partly let out in lodgings on a very modest street. It really did not matter about any of those things though, and she and Maxwell's mother got on very well after the first plunge, though the country doctor's widow was distinctly a country person, with the narrow social horizons of a villager whose knowledge of the city was confined to the compass of her courageous ventures in it.

To her own mother Louise feigned to see nothing repulsive in the humility of these. She had been rather fastidiously worldly, she had been even aggressively worldly, in her preference for a luxurious and tasteful setting, and her mother now found it hard to bear her contented acceptance of the pervading commonness of things at Mrs. Maxwell's. Either her senses were holden by her fondness for Maxwell, or else she was trying to hoodwink her mother by an effect of indifference; but Mrs. Hilary herself was certainly not obtuse to that commonness. If she did not rub it into Louise, which would have done no good, she did rub it into Louise's father, though that could hardly have been said to do any good either. Her report of the whole affair made him writhe, but when she had made him writhe enough she began to admit some extenuating circumstances. If Mrs. Maxwell was a country person, she was not foolish. She did not chant, in a vain attempt to be genteel in her speech; she did not expand unduly under Mrs. Hilary's graciousness, and she did not resent it. In fact, the graciousness had been very skilfully managed, and Mrs. Maxwell had not been allowed to feel that there was any condescension to her. She got on with Louise very well; if Mrs. Maxwell had any overweening pride in her son, she kept it as wholly to herself as any overweening pride she might have had in her son's choice.

Mrs. Hilary did not like her daughter's choice, but she had at last reached such resignation concerning it as the friends of a hopeless invalid may feel when the worst comes. She had tried to stop the affair when there was some hope or some use in trying, and now she determined to make the best of it. The worst was that Maxwell was undoubtedly of different origin and breeding, and he would always, in society, subject Louise to a consciousness of his difference if he did nothing more. But when you had said this, you seemed to have said all there was to say against him. The more the Hilarys learned about the young fellow the more reason they had to respect him. His life, on its level, was blameless. Every one who knew him spoke well of him, and those who knew him best spoke enthusiastically; he had believers in his talent and in his character. In a society so barometrical as ours, even in a city where it was the least barometrical, the obstacles to the acceptance of Maxwell were mainly subjective. They were formed not so much of what people would say as of what Mrs. Hilary felt they had a right to say, and, in view of the necessities of the case, she found herself realizing that if they did not say anything to her it would be much as if they had not said anything at all. She dealt with the fact before her frankly, and in the duties which it laid upon her she began to like Maxwell before Hilary did. Not that Hilary disliked him, but there was something in the young fellow taking his daughter away from him, in that cool matter-of-fact way, as if it were quite in the course of nature that he should, instead of being abashed and overwhelmed by his good fortune, which left Hilary with a misgiving lest he might realize it less and less as time went on.

W. D. Howells

Hilary had no definite ambition for her in marriage, but his vague dreams for her were not of a young man who meant to leave off being a newspaper writer to become a writer of plays. He instinctively wished her to be of his own order of things; and it had pleased him when he heard from his wife's report that Louise had seen the folly of her fancy for the young journalist whom a series of accidents had involved with their lives, and had decided to give him up. When the girl decided again, more tacitly, that she could not give him up, Hilary submitted, as he would have submitted to anything she wished. To his simple idolatry of her she was too good for anything on earth, and if he were to lose her, he found that after all he had no great choice in the matter. As soon as her marriage appeared inevitable, he agreed with his wife that their daughter must never have any unhappiness of their making; and they let her reverse without a word the purpose of going to spend the winter abroad which they had formed at her wish when she renounced Maxwell.

All this was still recent in point of time, and though marriage had remanded it to an infinite distance apparently with the young people, it had not yet taken away the importance or the charm of the facts and the feelings that had seemed the whole of life before marriage. When Louise turned from her retrospect she went in through the window that opened on the veranda and stood beside her husband, where he sat with his manuscript before him, frowning at it in the lamplight that made her blink a little after the dark outside. She put her hand on his head, and carried it down his cheek over his mouth, so that he might kiss its palm.

"Going to work much longer, little man?" she asked, and she kissed the top of his head in her turn. It always amused her to find how smooth and soft his hair was. He flung his pen away and threw himself back in his chair. "Oh, it's that infernal love business!" he said.

She sat down and let her hands fall on her lap. "Why, what makes it so hard?"

"Oh, I don't know. But it seems as if I were *fighting* it, as the actors say, all the way. It doesn't go of itself at all. It's forced, from the beginning."

"Why do you have it in, then?"

"I have to have it in. It has to be in every picture of life, as it has to be in every life. Godolphin is perfectly right. I talked with him about leaving it out to-day, but I had to acknowledge that it wouldn't do. In fact, I was the first to suggest that there must be some sort of love business when I first talked the play over with him. But I wish there hadn't. It makes me sick every time I touch it. The confounded fools don't know what to do with their love."

"They might get married with it," Louise suggested.

"I don't believe they have sense enough to think of that," said her husband. "The curse of their origin is on them, I suppose. I tried to imagine them when I was only fit to imagine a man hating a woman with all his might."

Louise laughed out her secure delight. "If the public could only know why your lovers were such feeble folk it would make the fortune of the play."

Maxwell laughed, too. "Yes, fancy Pinney getting hold of a fact like that and working it up with all his native delicacy in the Sunday edition of the *Events*!"

Pinney was a reporter of Maxwell's acquaintance, who stood to Louise for all that was most terrible in journalistic enterprise. "Don't!" she shrieked.

Maxwell went on. "He would have both our portraits in, and your father's and mother's, and my mother's; and your house on Commonwealth Avenue, and our meek mansion on Pinckney Street. He would make it a work of art, Pinney would, and he would believe that we were all secretly gratified with it, no matter how we pretended to writhe under it." He laughed and laughed, and then suddenly he stopped and was very grave.

"I know what you're thinking of now," said his wife.

"What?"

"Whether you couldn't use *our* affair in the play?"

"You're a witch! Yes, I was! I was thinking it wouldn't do."

"Stuff! It *will* do, and you must use it. Who would ever know it? And I shall not care how blackly you show me up. I deserve it. If I was the cause of your hating love so much that you failed with your lovers on the old lines, I certainly ought to be willing to be the means of your succeeding on lines that had never been tried before."

"Generous girl!" He bent over—he had not to bend far—and kissed her. Then he rose excitedly and began to walk the floor, with his hands in his pockets, and his head dropped forward. He broke into speech: "I could disguise it so that nobody would ever dream of it. I'll just take a hint from ourselves. How would it do to have had the girl actually reject him? It never came to that with us; and instead of his being a howling outside swell that was rather condescending to her, suppose I have him some sort of subordinate in her father's business? It doesn't matter much what; it's easy to arrange such a detail. She could be in love with him all the time, without even knowing it herself, or, at least, not knowing it when he offers himself; and she could always be vaguely hoping or expecting that he would come to time again."

"That's what I did," said his wife, "and you hadn't offered yourself either."

Maxwell stopped, with an air of discomfiture and disappointment. "You wouldn't like me to use that point, then?"

"What a simpleton! Of course I should! I shouldn't care if all the world knew it."

"Ah, well, we won't give it to Pinney, anyway; but I really think it could be done without involving our own facts. I should naturally work farther and farther away from them when the thing got to spinning. Just take a little color from them now and then. I might have him hating her all the way through, or, supposing he hated her, and yet doing all sorts of nice little things, and noble big things for her, till it came out about her father's crime, and then—" He stopped again with a certain air of distaste.

"That would be rather romantic, wouldn't it?" his wife asked.

"That was what I was thinking," he answered. "It would be confoundedly romantic."

"Well, I'll tell you," said Louise; "you could have them squabbling all the way through, and doing hateful things to one another."

"That would give it the cast of comedy."

"Well?"

W. D. Howells

"And that wouldn't do either."

"Not if it led up to the pathos and prettiness of their reconciliation in the end? Shakespeare mixes the comic and the tragic all through!"

"Oh yes, I know that—"

"And it would be very effective to leave the impression of their happiness with the audience, so that they might have strength to get on their rubbers and wraps after the tremendous ordeal of your Haxard death-scene."

"Godolphin wouldn't stand that. He wants the gloom of Haxard's death to remain in unrelieved inkiness at the end. He wants the people to go away thinking of Godolphin, and how well he did the last gasp. He wouldn't stand any love business there. He would rather not have any in the play."

"Very well, if you're going to be a slave to Godolphin—"

"I'm not going to be a slave to Godolphin, and if I can see my way to make the right use of such a passage at the close I'll do it even if it kills the play or Godolphin."

"Now you're shouting," said Louise. She liked to use a bit of slang when it was perfectly safe—as in very good company, or among those she loved; at other times she scrupulously shunned it.

"But I can do it somehow," Maxwell mused aloud. "Now I have the right idea, I can make it take any shape or color I want. It's magnificent!"

"And who thought of it?" she demanded.

"Who? Why, *I* thought of it myself."

"Oh, you little wretch!" she cried, in utter fondness, and she ran at him and drove him into a corner. "Now, say that again and I'll tickle you."

"No, no, no!" he laughed, and he fought away the pokes and thrusts she was aiming at him. "We both thought of it together. It was mind transference!"

She dropped her hands with an instant interest in the psychological phenomena. "Wasn't it strange? Or, no, it wasn't, either! If our lives are so united in everything, the wonder is that we don't think more things and say more things together. But now I want you to own, Brice, that I was the first to speak about your using our situation!"

"Yes, you were, and I was the first to think of it. But that's perfectly natural. You always speak of things before you think, and I always think of things before I speak."

"Well, I don't care," said Louise, by no means displeased with the formulation. "I shall always say it was perfectly miraculous. And I want you to give me credit for letting you have the idea after you had thought of it."

"Yes, there's nothing mean about you, Louise, as Pinney would say. By Jove, I'll bring Pinney in! I'll have Pinney interview Haxard concerning Greenshaw's disappearance."

"Very well, then, if you bring Pinney in, you will leave me out," said Louise. "I won't be in the same play with Pinney."

"Well, I won't bring Pinney in, then," said Maxwell. "I prefer you to Pinney—in a play. But I have got to have in an interviewer. It will be splendid on the stage, and I'll be the first to have him." He went and sat down at his table.

"You're not going to work any more to-night!" his wife protested.

"No, just jot down a note or two, to clinch that idea of ours in the right shape." He dashed off a few lines with pencil in his play at several points, and then he said: "There! I guess I shall get some bones into those two flabby idiots to-morrow. I see just how I can do it." He looked up and met his wife's adoring eyes.

"You're wonderful, Brice!" she said.

"Well, don't tell me so," he returned, "or it might spoil me. Now I wouldn't tell you how good you were, on any account."

"Oh yes, do, dearest!" she entreated, and a mist came into her eyes. "I don't think you praise me enough."

"How much ought I to praise you?"

"You ought to say that you think I'll never be a hinderance to you."

"Let me see," he said, and he pretended to reflect. "How would it do to say that if I ever come to anything worth while, it'll be because you made me?"

"Oh, Brice! But would it be true?" She dropped on her knees at his side.

"Well, I don't know. Let's hope it would," and with these words he laughed again and put his arms round her. Presently she felt his arm relax, and she knew that he had ceased to think about her and was thinking about his play again.

She pulled away, and "Well?" she asked.

He laughed at being found out so instantly. "That was a mighty good thing your father said when you went to tell him of our engagement."

"It was *very* good. But if you think I'm going to let you use *that* you're very much mistaken. No, Brice! Don't you touch papa. He wouldn't like it; he wouldn't understand it. Why, what a perfect cormorant you are!"

They laughed over his voracity, and he promised it should be held in check as to the point which he had thought for a moment might be worked so effectively into the play.

The next morning Louise said to her husband: "I can see, Brice, that you are full of the notion of changing that love business, and if I stay round I shall simply bother. I'm going down to lunch with papa and mamma, and get back here in the afternoon, just in time to madden Godolphin with my meddling."

She caught the first train after breakfast, and in fifteen minutes she was at Beverly Farms. She walked over to her father's cottage, where she found him smoking his cigar on the veranda.

He was alone; he said her mother had gone to Boston for the day; and he asked: "Did you walk from the station? Why didn't you come back in the carriage? It had just been there with your mother."

"I didn't see it. Besides, I might not have taken it if I had. As

W. D. Howells

the wife of a struggling young playwright, I should have probably thought it unbecoming to drive. But the struggle is practically over, you'll be happy to know."

"What? Has he given it up?" asked her father.

"Given it up! He's just got a new light on his love business!"

"I thought his love business had gone pretty well with him," said Hilary, with a lingering grudge in his humor.

"This is another love business!" Louise exclaimed. "The love business in the play. Brice has always been so disgusted with it that he hasn't known what to do. But last night we thought it out together, and I've left him this morning getting his hero and heroine to stand on their legs without being held up. Do you want to know about it?"

"I think I can get on without," said Hilary.

Louise laughed joyously. "Well, you wouldn't understand what a triumph it was if I told you. I suppose, papa, you've no idea how Philistine you are. But you're nothing to mamma!"

"I dare say," said Hilary, sulkily. But she looked at him with eyes beaming with gayety, and he could see that she was happy, and he was glad at heart. "When does Maxwell expect to have his play done?" he relented so far as to ask.

"Why, it's done now, and has been for a month, in one sense, and it isn't done at all in another. He has to keep working it over, and he has to keep fighting Godolphin's inspirations. He comes over from Manchester with a fresh lot every afternoon."

"I dare say Maxwell will be able to hold his own," said Hilary, but not so much proudly as dolefully.

She knew he was braving it out about the theatre, and that secretly he thought it undignified, and even disreputable, to be connected with it, or to be in such close relations with an actor as Maxwell seemed to be with this fellow who talked of taking his play. Hilary could go back very easily to the time in Boston when the theatres were not allowed open on Saturday night, lest they should profane the approaching Sabbath, and when you would no more have seen an actor in society than an elephant. He had not yet got used to meeting them, and he always felt his difference, though he considered himself a very liberal man, and was fond of the theatre— from the front.

He asked now, "What sort of chap is he, really?" meaning Godolphin, and Louise did her best to reassure him. She told him Godolphin was young and enthusiastic; and he had an ideal of the drama; and he believed in Brice; and he had been two seasons with Booth and Barrett; and now he had made his way on the Pacific Coast, and wanted a play that he could take the road with. She parroted those phrases, which made her father's flesh creep, and she laughed when she saw it creeping, for sympathy; her own had crept first.

"Well," he said, at last, "he won't expect you and Maxwell to take the road too with it?"

"Oh no, we shall only be with him in New York. He won't put the play on there first; they usually try a new play in the country."

"Oh, do they?" said Hilary, with a sense that his daughter's knowledge of the fact was disgraceful to her.

"Yes. Shall I tell you what they call that? Trying it on a dog!" she shrieked, and Hilary had to laugh, too. "It's dreadful," she went on. "Then, if it doesn't kill the dog, Godolphin will bring it to New York, and put it on for a run—a week or a month—as long as his money holds out. If he believes in it, he'll fight it." Her father looked at her for explanation, and she said, with a gleeful perception of his suffering, "He'll keep it on if he has to play to paper every night. That is, to free tickets."

"Oh!" said Hilary. "And are you to be there the whole time with him?"

"Why, not necessarily. But Brice will have to be there for the rehearsals; and if we are going to live in New York—"

Hilary sighed. "I wish Maxwell was going on with his newspaper work; I might be of use to him in that line, if he were looking forward to an interest in a newspaper; but I couldn't buy him a theatre, you know."

Louise laughed. "He wouldn't let you buy him anything, papa; Brice is awfully proud. Now, I'll tell you, if you want to know, just how we expect to manage in New York; Brice and I have been talking it all over; and it's all going to be done on that thousand dollars he saved up from his newspaper work, and we're not going to touch a cent of my money till that is gone. Don't you call that pretty business-like?"

"Very," said Hilary, and he listened with apparent acquiescence to the details of a life which he divined that Maxwell had planned from his own simple experience. He did not like the notion of it for his daughter, but he could not help himself, and it was a consolation to see that she was in love with it.

She went back from it to the play itself, and told her father that now Maxwell had got the greatest love business for it that there ever was. She would not explain just what it was, she said, because her father would get a wrong notion of it if she did. "But I have a great mind to tell you something else," she said, "if you think you can behave sensibly about it, papa. Do you suppose you can?"

Hilary said he would try, and she went on: "It's part of the happiness of having got hold of the right kind of love business now, and I don't know but it unconsciously suggested it to both of us, for we both thought of the right thing at the same time; but in the beginning you couldn't have told it from a quarrel." Her father started, and Louise began to laugh. "Yes, we had quite a little tiff, just like *real* married people, about my satirizing one of Godolphin's inspirations to his face, and wounding his feelings. Brice is so cautious and so gingerly with him; and he was vexed with me, and told me he wished I wouldn't do it; and that vexed me, and I said I wouldn't have anything to do with his play after this; and I didn't speak to him again till after supper. I said he was self-centred, and he *is*. He's always thinking about his play and its chances; and I suppose I would rather have had him think more about me now and then. But I've discovered a way now, and I believe it will serve the same purpose. I'm going to enter so fully into his work that I shall be part of it; and when he is thinking of that he will be thinking of me without knowing it. Now, you wouldn't say there was anything in that to cry about, would you? and yet you see I'm at it!" and with this she suddenly dropped her face on her father's shoulder.

Hilary groaned in his despair of being able to imagine an injury sufficiently atrocious to inflict on Maxwell for having brought this grief upon his girl. At the sound of his groan, as if she perfectly interpreted his meaning in it, she broke from

W. D. Howells

a sob into a laugh. "Will you never," she said, dashing away the tears, "learn to let me cry, simply because I am a goose, papa, and a goose must weep without reason, because she feels like it? I won't have you thinking that I am not the happiest person in the world; and I was, even when I was suffering so because I had to punish Brice for telling me I had done wrong. And if you think I'm not, I will never tell you anything more, for I see you can't be trusted. Will you?"

He said no to her rather complicated question, and he was glad to believe that she was really as happy as she declared, for if he could not have believed it, he would have had to fume away an intolerable deal of exasperation. This always made him very hot and uncomfortable, and he shrank from it, but he would have done it if it had been necessary. As it was, he got back to his newspaper again with a sufficiently light heart, when Louise gave him a final kiss, and went indoors and put herself in authority for the day, and ordered what she liked for luncheon. The maids were delighted to have her, and she had a welcome from them all, which was full of worship for her as a bride whose honeymoon was not yet over.

She went away before her mother got home, and she made her father own, before she left him, that he had never had such a lovely day since he could remember. He wanted to drive over to Magnolia with her; but she accused him of wanting to go so that he could spy round a little, and satisfy himself of the misery of her married life; and then he would not insist.

IV

Louise kept wondering, the whole way back, how Maxwell had managed the recasting of the love-business, and she wished she had stayed with him, so that he could have appealed to her at any moment on the points that must have come up all the time. She ought to have coached him more fully about it, and told him the woman's side of such a situation, as he never could have imagined how many advances a woman can make with a man in such an affair and the man never find it out. She had not made any advances herself when she wished to get him back, but she had wanted to make them; and she knew he would not have noticed it if she had done the boldest sort of things to encourage him, to let him know that she liked him; he was so simple, in his straightforward egotism, beside her sinuous unselfishness.

She began to think how she was always contriving little sacrifices to his vanity, his modesty, and he was always accepting them with a serene ignorance of the fact that they were offered; and at this she strayed off on a little by-way in her revery, and thought how it was his mind, always, that charmed her; it was no ignoble fondness she felt; no poor, grovelling pleasure in his good looks, though she had always seen that in a refined sort he had a great deal of manly beauty. But she had held her soul aloof from all that, and

W. D. Howells

could truly say that what she adored in him was the beauty of his talent, which he seemed no more conscious of than of his dreamy eyes, the scornful sweetness of his mouth, the purity of his forehead, his sensitive nostrils, his pretty, ineffective little chin. She had studied her own looks with reference to his, and was glad to own them in no wise comparable, though she knew she was more graceful, and she could not help seeing that she was a little taller; she kept this fact from herself as much as possible. Her features were not regular, like his, but she could perceive that they had charm in their irregularity; she could only wonder whether he thought that line going under her chin, and suggesting a future double chin in the little fold it made, was so very ugly. He seemed never to have thought of her looks, and if he cared for her, it was for some other reason, just as she cared for him. She did not know what the reason could be, but perhaps it was her sympathy, her appreciation, her cheerfulness; Louise believed that she had at least these small merits.

The thought of them brought her back to the play again, and to the love-business, and she wondered how she could have failed to tell him, when they were talking about what should bring the lovers together, after their prefatory quarrel, that simply willing it would do it. She knew that after she began to wish Maxwell back, she was in such a frenzy that she believed her volition brought him back; and now she really believed that you could hypnotize fate in some such way, and that your longings would fulfil themselves if they were intense enough. If he could not use that idea in this play, then he ought to use it in some other, something psychological, symbolistic, Maeterlinckish.

She was full of it when she dismounted from the barge at the hotel and hurried over to their cottage, and she was intolerably disappointed when she did not find him at work in the parlor.

"Brice! Brice!" she shouted, in the security of having the whole cottage to herself. She got no answer, and ran up to their room, overhead. He was not there, either, and now it seemed but too probable that he had profited by her absence to go out for a walk alone, after his writing, and fallen from the rocks, and been killed—he was so absent-minded. She offered a vow to Heaven that if he were restored to her she would never leave him again, even for a half-day, as long as either of them lived. In reward for this she saw him coming from the direction of the beach, where nothing worse could have befallen him than a chill from the water, if the wind was off shore and he had been taking a bath.

She had not put off her hat yet, and she went out to meet him; she could not kiss him at once, if she went to meet him, but she could wait till she got back to the cottage, and then kiss him. It would be a trial to wait, but it would be a trial to wait for him to come in, and he might stroll off somewhere else, unless she went to him. As they approached each other she studied his face for some sign of satisfaction with his morning's work. It lighted up at sight of her, but there remained an inner dark in it to her eye.

"What is the matter?" she asked, as she put her hand through his arm, and hung forward upon it so that she could look up into his face. "How did you get on with the love-business?"

"Oh, I think I've got that all right," he answered, with a certain reservation. "I've merely blocked it out, of course."

"So that you can show it to Godolphin?"

"I guess so."

"I see that you're not sure of it. We must go over it before he comes. He hasn't been here yet?"

W. D. Howells

"Not yet."

"Why are you so quiet, Brice? Is anything the matter? You look tired."

"I'm not particularly tired."

"Then you are worried. What is it?"

"Oh, you would have to know, sooner or later." He took a letter from his pocket and gave it to her. "It came just after I had finished my morning's work."

She pulled it out of the envelope and read:

"MANCHESTER-BY-THE-SEA, Friday.

"DEAR SIR: I beg leave to relinquish any claim that you may feel I have established to the play you have in hand. As it now stands, I do not see my part in it, and I can imagine why you should be reluctant to make further changes in it, in order to meet my requirements.

"If I can be of any service to you in placing the piece, I shall be glad to have you make use of me.

"Yours truly,
"LAUNCELOT GODOLPHIN."

"You blame *me*!" she said, after a blinding moment, in which the letter darkened before her eyes, and she tottered in her walk. She gave it back to him as she spoke.

"What a passion you have for blaming!" he answered, coldly. "If I fixed the blame on you it wouldn't help."

"No," Louise meekly assented, and they walked along towards their cottage. They hardly spoke again before they reached it and went in. Then she asked, "Did you expect anything like this from the way he parted with you yesterday?"

Maxwell gave a bitter laugh. "From the way we parted yesterday I was expecting him early this afternoon, with the world in the palm of his hand, to lay it at my feet. He all but fell upon my neck when he left me. I suppose his not actually doing it was an actor's intimation that we were to see each other no more."

"I wish you had nothing to do with actors!" said Louise.

"*They* appear to have nothing to do with me," said Maxwell. "It comes to the same thing."

They reached the cottage, and sat down in the little parlor where she had left him so hopefully at work in the morning, where they had talked his play over so jubilantly the night before.

"What are you going to do?" she asked, after an abysmal interval.

"Nothing. What is there to do?"

"You have a right to an explanation; you ought to demand it."

"I don't need any explanation. The case is perfectly clear. Godolphin doesn't want my play. That is all."

"Oh, Brice!" she lamented. "I am so dreadfully sorry, and I know it was my fault. Why don't you let me write to him, and explain—"

Maxwell shook his head. "He doesn't want any explanation. He doesn't want the play, even. We must make up our minds to that, and let him go. Now we can try it with your managers."

Louise felt keenly the unkindness of his calling them her managers, but she was glad to have him unkind to her; deep within her Unitarianism she had the Puritan joy in suffering for a sin; her treatment of Godolphin's suggestion of a skirt-dance, while very righteous in itself, was a sin against her husband's interest, and she would rather he were unkind to her than not. The sooner she was punished for it and done with it, the better; in her unscientific conception of life, the consequences of a sin ended with its punishment. If Maxwell had upbraided her with the bitterness she merited, it would have been to her as if it were all right again with Godolphin. His failure to do so left the injury unrepaired, and she would have to do something. "I suppose you don't care to let me see what you've written to-day?"

"No, not now," said Maxwell, in a tone that said, "I haven't the heart for it."

They sat awhile without speaking, and then she ventured, "Brice, I have an idea, but I don't know what you will think of it. Why not take Godolphin's letter on the face of it, and say that you are very sorry he must give up the play, and that you will be greatly obliged to him if he can suggest some other actor? That would be frank, at least."

Maxwell broke into a laugh that had some joy in it. "Do you think so? It isn't my idea of frankness exactly."

"No, of course not. You always say what you mean, and you

don't change. That is what is so beautiful in you. You can't understand a nature that is one thing to-day and another thing to-morrow."

"Oh, I think I can," said Maxwell, with a satirical glance.

"Brice!" she softly murmured; and then she said, "Well, I don't care. He *is* just like a woman."

"You didn't like my saying so last night."

"That was a different thing. At any rate, it's I that say so now, and I want you to write that to him. It will bring him back flying. Will you?"

"I'll think about it," said Maxwell; "I'm not sure that I want Godolphin back, or not at once. It's a great relief to be rid of him, in a certain way, though a manager might be worse slavery. Still, I think I would like to try a manager. I have never shown this play to one, and I know the Odeon people in Boston, and, perhaps—"

"You are saying that to comfort me."

"I wouldn't comfort you for worlds, my dear. I am saying this to distress you. But since I have worked that love-business over, it seems to me much less a one-part play, and if I could get a manager to take a fancy to it I could have my own way with it much better; at least, he wouldn't want me to take all the good things out of the other characters' mouths and stuff them into Haxard's."

"Do you really think so?"

"I really thought so before I got Godolphin's letter. That made him seem the one and only man for me."

"Yes," Louise assented, with a sad intelligence.

Maxwell seemed to have got some strength from confronting his calamity. At any rate, he said, almost cheerfully, "I'll read you what I wrote this morning," and she had to let him, though she felt that it was taking her at a moment when her wish to console him was so great that she would not be able to criticise him. But she found that he had done it so well there was no need of criticism.

"You are wonderful, Brice!" she said, in a transport of adoration, which she indulged as simply his due. "You are miraculous! Well, this is the greatest triumph yet, even of *your* genius. How you have seized the whole idea! And so subtly, so delicately! And so completely disguised! The girl acts just as a girl *would* have acted. How could you know it?"

"Perhaps I've seen it," he suggested, demurely.

"No, no, you *didn't* see it! That is the amusing part of it. You were as blind as a bat all the time, and you never had the least suspicion; you've told me so."

"Well, then, I've seen it retrospectively."

"Perhaps that way. But I don't believe you've seen it at all. You've divined it; and that's where your genius is worth all the experience in the world. The girl is twice as good as the man, and you never experienced a girl's feelings or motives. You divined them. It's pure inspiration. It's the prophet in you!"

"You'll be stoning me next," said Maxwell. "I don't think the man is so very bad, even if I didn't divine him."

"Yes, for a poor creature of experience and knowledge, he will do very well. But he doesn't compare with the girl."

"I hadn't so good a model."

She hugged him for saying that. "You pay the prettiest compliments in the world, even if you don't pick up handkerchiefs."

Their joy in the triumph of his art was unalloyed by the hope of anything outside of it, of any sort of honor or profit from it, though they could not keep the thought of these out very long.

"Yes," she said, after one of the delicious silences that divided their moments of exaltation. "There won't be any trouble about getting your play taken, *now*."

After supper they strolled down for the sunset and twilight on the rocks. There, as the dusk deepened, she put her wrap over his shoulders as well as her own, and pulled it together in front of them both. "I am not going to have you taking cold, now, when you need all your health for your work more than ever. That love-business seems to me perfect just as it is, but I know you won't be satisfied till you have put the very last touch on it."

"Yes, I see all sorts of things I can do to it. Louise!"

"Well, what?"

"Don't you see that the love-business is the play now? I have got to throw away all the sin-interest, all the Haxard situation, or keep them together as they are, and write a new play altogether, with the light, semi-comic motive of the love-business for the motive of the whole. It's out of tone

W. D. Howells

with Haxard's tragedy, and it can't be brought into keeping with it. The sin-interest will kill the love-business, or the love-business will kill the sin-interest. Don't you see?"

"Why, of course! You must make this light affair now, and when it's opened the way for you with the public you can bring out the old play," she assented, and it instantly became the old play in both their minds; it became almost the superannuated play. They talked it over in this new aspect, and then they went back to the cottage, to look at the new play as it shadowed itself forth in the sketch Maxwell had made. He read the sketch to her again, and they saw how it could be easily expanded to three or four acts, and made to fill the stage and the evening.

"And it will be the most original thing that ever was!" she exulted.

"I don't think there's been anything exactly like it before," he allowed.

From time to time they spoke to each other in the night, and she asked if he were asleep, and he if she were asleep, and then they began to talk of the play again. Towards morning they drowsed a little, but at their time of life the loss of a night's sleep means nothing, and they rose as glad as they had lain down.

"I'll tell you, Brice," she said, the first thing, "you must have it that they have been engaged, and you can call the play 'The Second Chapter,' or something more alliterative. Don't you think that would be a good name?"

"It would make the fortune of any play," he answered, "let alone a play of such merit as this."

"Well, then, sha'n't you always say that I did something towards it?"

"I shall say you did everything towards it. You originated the idea, and named it, and I simply acted as your amanuensis, as it were, and wrote it out mostly from your dictation. It shall go on the bills, 'The Second Chapter,' a demi-semi-serious comedy by Mrs. Louise Hilary Maxwell—in letters half a foot high—and by B. Maxwell—in very small lower case, that can't be read without the aid of a microscope."

"Oh, Brice! If you make him talk that way to her, it will be perfectly killing."

"I dare say the audience will find it so."

They were so late at breakfast, and sat there so long talking, for Maxwell said he did not feel like going to work quite so promptly as usual, that it was quite ten o'clock when they came out of the dining-room, and then they stayed awhile gossiping with people on the piazza of the hotel before they went back to their cottage. When they came round the corner in sight of it they saw the figure of a man pacing back and forth on the veranda, with his head dropped forward, and swinging a stick thoughtfully behind him. Louise pulled Maxwell convulsively to a halt, for the man was Godolphin.

"What do you suppose it means?" she gasped.

"I suppose he will tell us," said Maxwell, dryly. "Don't stop and stare at him. He has got eyes all over him, and he's clothed with self-consciousness as with a garment, and I don't choose to let him think that his being here is the least important or surprising."

"No, of course not. That would be ridiculous," and she would have liked to pause for a moment's worship of her husband's sense, which appeared to her almost as great as his genius. But it seemed to her an inordinately long time before they reached the cottage-gate, and Godolphin came half-way down the walk to meet them.

He bowed seriously to her, and then said, with dignity, to her husband, "Mr. Maxwell, I feel that I owe you an apology—or an explanation, rather—for the abrupt note I sent you yesterday. I wish to assure you that I had no feeling in the matter, and that I am quite sincere in my offer of my services."

"Why, you're very good, Mr. Godolphin," said Maxwell. "I knew that I could fully rely on your kind offer. Won't you come in?" He offered the actor his hand, and they moved together towards the cottage; Louise had at once gone before, but not so far as to be out of hearing.

"Why, thank you, I *will* sit down a moment. I found the walk over rather fatiguing. It's going to be a hot day." He passed his handkerchief across his forehead, and insisted upon placing a chair for Mrs. Maxwell before he could be made to sit down, though she said that she was going indoors, and would not sit. "You understand, of course, Mr. Maxwell, that I should still like to have your play, if it could be made what I want?"

Maxwell would not meet his wife's eye in answering. "Oh, yes; the only question with me is, whether I can make it what you want. That has been the trouble all along. I know that the love-business in the play, as it stood, was inadequate. But yesterday, just before I got your note, I had been working it over in a perfectly new shape. I wish, if you have a quarter of an hour to throw away, you'd let me show you what I've written. Perhaps you can advise me."

"Why, I shall be delighted to be of any sort of use, Mr. Maxwell," said Godolphin, with softened state; and he threw himself back in his chair with an air of eager readiness.

"I will get your manuscript, Brice," said Louise, at a motion her husband made to rise. She ran in and brought it out, and then went away again. She wished to remain somewhere within earshot, but, upon the whole, she decided against it, and went upstairs, where she kept herself from eavesdropping by talking with the chambermaid, who had come over from the hotel.

V

Louise did not come down till she heard Godolphin walking away on the plank. She said to herself that she had ship-wrecked her husband once by putting in her oar, and she was not going to do it again. When the actor's footfalls died out in the distance she descended to the parlor, where she found Maxwell over his manuscript at the table.

She had to call to him, "Well?" before he seemed aware of her presence.

Even then he did not look round, but he said, "Godolphin wants to play Atland."

"The lover?"

"Yes. He thinks he sees his part in it."

"And do you?"

"How do I know?"

"Well, I am glad I let him get safely away before I came back, for I certainly couldn't have held in when he proposed that, if I had been here. I don't understand you, Brice! Why do you have anything more to do with him? Why do you let him touch the new play? Was he ever of the least use with the old one?"

Maxwell lay back in his chair with a laugh. "Not the least in the world." The realization of the fact amused him more and more. "I was just thinking how everything he ever got me to do to it," he looked down at the manuscript, "was false and wrong. They talk about a knowledge of the stage as if the stage were a difficult science, instead of a very simple piece of mechanism whose limitations and possibilities any one can seize at a glance. All that their knowledge of it comes to is clap-trap, pure and simple. They brag of its resources, and tell you the carpenter can do anything you want nowadays, but if you attempt anything outside of their tradition they are frightened. They think that their exits and their entrances are great matters, and that they must come on with such a speech, and go off with such another; but it is not of the least consequence how they come or go if they have something interesting to say or do."

"Why don't you say these things to Godolphin?"

"I do, and worse. He admits their truth with a candor and an intelligence that are dismaying. He has a perfect conception of Atland's part, and he probably will play it in a way to set your teeth on edge."

"Why do you let him? Why don't you keep your play and offer it to a manager or some actor who will know how to do it?" demanded Louise, with sorrowful submission.

"Godolphin will know how to do it, even if he isn't able to. And, besides, I should be a fool to fling him away for any sort of promising uncertainty."

"He was willing to fling you away!"

"Yes, but I'm not so important to him as he is to me. He's the best I can do for the present. It's a compromise all the way through—a cursed spite from beginning to end. Your own words don't represent your ideas, and the more conscience you put into the work the further you get from what you thought it would be. Then comes the actor with the infernal chemistry of his personality. He imagines the thing perfectly, not as you imagined it, but as you wrote it, and then he is no more able to play it as he imagined it than you were to write it as you imagined it. What the public finally gets is something three times removed from the truth that was first in the dramatist's mind. But I'm very lucky to have Godolphin back again."

"I hope you're not going to let him see that you think so."

"Oh, no! I'm going to keep him in a suppliant attitude throughout, and I'm going to let you come in and tame his spirit, if he—kicks."

"Don't be vulgar, Brice," said Louise, and she laughed rather forlornly. "I don't see how you have the heart to joke, if you think it's so bad as you say."

"I haven't. I'm joking without any heart." He stood up. "Let us go and take a bath."

She glanced at him with a swift inventory of his fagged looks, and said, "Indeed, you shall not take a bath this morning. You couldn't react against it. You won't, will you?"

"No, I'll only lie on the sand, if you can pick me out a good warm spot, and watch you."

"I shall not bathe, either."

"Well, then, I'll watch the other women." He put out his hand and took hers.

She felt his touch very cold. "You are excited I can see. I wish—"

"What? That I was not an intending dramatist?"

"That you didn't have such excitements in your life. They will kill you."

"They are all that will keep me alive."

They went down to the beach, and walked back and forth on its curve several times before they dropped in the sand at a discreet distance from several groups of hotel acquaintance. People were coming and going from the line of bath-houses that backed upon the low sand-bank behind them, with its tufts of coarse silvery-green grasses. The Maxwells bowed to some of the ladies who tripped gayly past them in their airy costumes to the surf, or came up from it sobered and shivering. Four or five young fellows, with sun-blackened arms and legs, were passing ball near them. A pony-carriage drove by on the wet sand; a horseman on a crop-tailed roan thumped after it at a hard trot. Dogs ran barking vaguely about, and children with wooden shovels screamed at their play. Far off shimmered the sea, of one pale blue with the sky. The rooks were black at either end of the beach; a line of sail-boats and dories swung across its crescent beyond the bathers, who bobbed up and down in the surf, or showed a head here and there outside of it.

"What a singular spectacle," said Maxwell. "The casting off of the conventional in sea-bathing always seems to me like the effect of those dreams where we appear in society insufficiently dressed, and wonder whether we can make it go."

"Yes, isn't it?" His wife tried to cover all the propositions with one loosely fitting assent.

"I'm surprised," Maxwell went on, "that some realistic wretch hasn't put this sort of thing on the stage. It would be tremendously effective; if he made it realistic enough it would be attacked by the press as improper and would fill the house. Couldn't we work a sea-bathing scene into the 'Second Chapter'? It would make the fortune of the play, and it would give Godolphin a chance to show his noble frame in something like the majesty of nature. Godolphin would like nothing better. We could have Atland rescue Salome, and Godolphin could flop round among the canvas breakers for ten minutes, and come on for a recall with the heroine, both dripping real water all over the stage."

"Don't be disgusting, Brice," said his wife, absently. She had her head half turned from him, watching a lady who had just come out of her bath-house and was passing very near them on her way to the water. Maxwell felt the inattention in his wife's tone and looked up.

The bather returned their joint gaze steadily from eyes that seemed, as Maxwell said, to smoulder under their long lashes, and to question her effect upon them in a way that he was some time finding a phrase for. He was tormented to make out whether she were a large person or not; without her draperies he could not tell. But she moved with splendid freedom, and her beauty expressed a maturity of experience beyond her years; she looked young, and yet she looked as if she had been taking care of herself a good while. She was certainly very handsome, Louise owned to herself, as the lady quickened her pace, and finally ran down to the water and plunged into a breaker that rolled in at the right moment in uncommon volume.

"Well?" she asked her husband, whose eyes had gone with hers.

"We ought to have clapped."

"Do you think she is an actress?"

"I don't know. I never saw her before. She seemed to turn the sunshine into lime-light as she passed. Why! that's rather pretty, isn't it? And it's a verse. I wonder what it is about these people. The best of them have nothing of the stage in them—at least, the men haven't. I'm not sure, though, that the women haven't. There are lots of women off the stage who are actresses, but they don't seem so. They're personal; this one was impersonal. She didn't seem to regard me as a man; she regarded me as a house. Did you feel that?"

"Yes, that was it, I suppose. But she regarded you more than she did me, I think."

"Why, of course. You were only a matinee."

They sat half an hour longer in the sand, and then he complained that the wind blew all the warmth out of him as fast as the sun shone it into him. She felt his hand next her and found it still cold; after a glance round she furtively felt his forehead.

"You're still thinking," she sighed. "Come! We must go back."

"Yes. That girl won't be out of the water for half an hour yet; and we couldn't wait to see her clothed and in her right mind afterwards."

"What makes you think she's a girl?" asked his wife, as they moved slowly off.

He did not seem to have heard her question. He said, "I don't believe I can make the new play go, Louise; I haven't the strength for it. There's too much good stuff in Haxard; I can't throw away what I've done on it."

"That is just what I was thinking, Brice! It would be too bad to lose that. The love-business as you've remodeled it is all very well. But it *is* light; it's comedy; and Haxard is such splendid tragedy. I want you to make your first impression in that. You can do comedy afterwards; but if you did comedy first, the public would never think your tragedy was serious."

"Yes, there's a law in that. A clown mustn't prophesy. If a prophet chooses to joke, now and then, all well and good. I couldn't begin now and expand that love-business into a whole play. It must remain an episode, and Godolphin must take it or leave it. Of course he'll want Atland emaciated to fatten Haxard, as he calls it. But Atland doesn't amount to much, as it is, and I don't believe I could make him; it's essentially a passive part; Salome must make the chief effect in that business, and I think I'll have her a little more serious, too. It'll be more in keeping with the rest."

"I don't see why she shouldn't be serious. There's nothing ignoble in what she does."

"No. It can be very impassioned."

Louise thought of the smouldering eyes of that woman, and she wondered if they were what suggested something very impassioned to Maxwell; but with all the frankness between them, she did not ask him.

On their way to the cottage they saw one of the hotel bell-boys coming out. "Just left a telegram in there for you," he called, as he came towards them.

Louise began, "Oh, dear, I hope there's nothing the matter with papa! Or your mother."

She ran forward, and Maxwell followed at his usual pace, so that she had time to go inside and come out with the despatch before he mounted the veranda steps.

"You open it!" she entreated, piteously, holding it towards him.

He pulled it impatiently open, and glanced at the signature. "It's from Godolphin;" and he read, "Don't destroy old play. Keep new love-business for episode. Will come over this afternoon." Maxwell smiled. "More mind transference."

Louise laughed in hysterical relief. "Now you can make him do just what you want."

VI

Maxwell, now, at least, knew that he had got his play going in the right direction again. He felt a fresh pleasure in returning to the old lines after his excursion in the region of comedy, and he worked upon them with fresh energy. He rehabilitated the love-business as he and his wife had newly imagined it, and, to disguise the originals the more effectively, he made the girl, whom he had provisionally called Salome, more like himself than Louise in certain superficial qualities, though in an essential nobleness and singleness, which consisted with a great deal of feminine sinuosity and subtlety, she remained a portrait of Louise. He was doubtful whether the mingling of characteristics would not end in unreality, but she was sure it would not; she said he was so much like a woman in the traits he had borrowed from himself that Salome would be all the truer for being like him; or, at any rate, she would be finer, and more ideal. She said that it was nonsense, the way people regarded women as altogether different from men; she believed they were very much alike; a girl was as much the daughter of her father as of her mother; she alleged herself as proof of the fact that a girl was often a great deal more her father's daughter, and she argued that if Maxwell made Salome quite in his own spiritual image, no one would dream of criticising her as unwomanly. Then he asked if he need only make Atland in her spiritual image to have him the manliest sort of fellow. She said that was not what she meant, and, in any case, a man could have feminine traits, and be all the nicer for them, but, if a woman had masculine traits, she would be disgusting. At the same time, if you drew a man from a woman, he would be ridiculous.

"Then you want me to model Atland on myself, too," said Maxwell.

She thought a moment. "Yes, I do. If Salome is to be taken mostly from me, I couldn't bear to have him like anybody but you. It would be indelicate."

"Well, now, I'll tell you what, I'm not going to stand it," said Maxwell. "I am going to make Atland like Pinney."

But she would not be turned from the serious aspect of the affair by his joking. She asked, "Do you think it would intensify the situation if he were not equal to her? If the spectator could be made to see that she was throwing herself away on him, after all?"

"Wouldn't that leave the spectator a little too inconsolable? You don't want the love-business to double the tragedy, you want to have it relieved, don't you?"

"Yes, that is true. You must make him worth all the sacrifice. I couldn't stand it if he wasn't."

Maxwell frowned, as he always did when he became earnest, and said with a little sigh, "He must be passive, negative, as I said; you must simply feel that he is *good*, and that she will be safe with him, after the worst has happened to her father. And I must keep the interest of the love-business light, without letting it become farcical. I must get charm, all I can, into her character. You won't mind my getting the charm all from you?"

"Oh, Brice, what sweet things you say to me! I wish everybody could know how divine you are."

"The women would all be making love to me, and I should hate that. One is quite enough."

"*Am* I quite enough?" she entreated.

"You have been up to the present time."

"And do you think I shall always be?" She slid from her chair to her knees on the floor beside him, where he sat at his desk, and put her arms round him.

He did not seem to know it. "Look here, Louise, I have got to connect this love-business with the main action of the play, somehow. It won't do simply to have it an episode. How would it do to have Atland know all the time that Haxard has killed Greenshaw, and be keeping it from Salome, while she is betraying her love for him?"

"Wouldn't that be rather tawdry?" Louise let her arms slip down to her side, and looked up at him, as she knelt.

"Yes, it would," he owned.

He looked very unhappy about it, and she rose to her feet, as if to give it more serious attention. "Brice, I want your play to be thoroughly honest and true from beginning to end, and not to have any sort of catchpenny effectivism in it. You have planned it so nobly that I can't bear to have you lower the standard the least bit; and I think the honest and true way is to let the love-business be a pleasant fact in the case, as it might very well be. Those things *do* keep going on in life alongside of the greatest misery, the greatest unhappiness."

"Well," said Maxwell, "I guess you are right about the love-business. I'll treat it frankly for what it is, a fact in the case. That will be the right way, and that will be the strong way. It will be like life. I don't know that you are bound to relate things strictly to each other in art, any more than they are related in life. There are all sorts of incidents and interests playing round every great event that seem to have no more relation to it than the rings of Saturn have to Saturn. They form the atmosphere of it. If I can let Haxard's wretchedness be seen at last through the atmosphere of his daughter's happiness!"

"Yes," she said, "that will be quite enough." She knew that they had talked up to the moment when he could best begin to work, and now left him to himself.

Within a week he got the rehabilitated love-business in place, and the play ready to show to Godolphin again. He had managed to hold the actor off in the meantime, but now he returned in full force, with suggestions and misgivings which had first to be cleared away before he could give a clear mind to what Maxwell had done. Then Maxwell could see that he was somehow disappointed, for he began to talk as if there were no understanding between them for his taking the play. He praised it warmly, but he said that it would be hard to find a woman to do the part of Salome.

"That is the principal part in the piece now, you know," he added.

"I don't see how," Maxwell protested. "It seems to me that her character throws Haxard's into greater relief than before, and gives it more prominence."

"You've made the love-business too strong, I think. I supposed you would have something light and graceful to occupy the house in the suspense between the points in Haxard's case. If I were to do him, I should be afraid that people would come back from Salome to him with more or less of an effort, I don't say they would, but that's the way it strikes me now; perhaps some one else would look at it quite differently."

"Then, as it is, you don't want it?"

"I don't say that. But it seems to me that Salome is the principal figure now. I think that's a mistake."

"If it's a fact, it's a mistake. I don't want to have it so," said Maxwell, and he made such effort as he could to swallow his disgust.

Godolphin asked, after a while, "In that last scene between her and her father, and in fact in all the scenes between them, couldn't you give more of the strong speeches to him? She's a great creation now, but isn't she too great for Atland?"

"I've kept Atland under, purposely, because the part is necessarily a negative one, and because I didn't want him to compete with Haxard at all."

"Yes, that is all right; but as it is, *she* competes with Haxard."

After Godolphin had gone, Louise came down, and found Maxwell in a dreary muse over his manuscript. He looked up at her with a lack-lustre eye, and said, "Godolphin is jealous of Salome now. What he really wants is a five-act monologue that will keep him on the stage all the time. He thinks that as it is, she will take all the attention from him."

Louise appeared to reflect. "Well, isn't there something in that?"

"Good heavens! I should think you were going to play Haxard, too!"

"No; but of course you can't have two characters of equal importance in your play. Some one has to be first, and Godolphin doesn't want an actress taking all the honors away from him."

"Then why did you pretend to like the way I had done it," Maxwell demanded, angrily, "if you think she will take the honors from him?"

"I didn't say that I did. All that I want is that you should ask yourself whether she would or not."

"Are *you* jealous of her?"

"Now, my dear, if you are going to be unreasonable, I will not talk with you."

Nothing maddened Maxwell so much as to have his wife take this tone with him, when he had followed her up through the sinuosities that always began with her after a certain point. Short of that she was as frank and candid as a man, and he understood her, but beyond that the eternal womanly began, and he could make nothing of her. She evaded, and came and went, and returned upon her course, and all with as good a conscience, apparently, as if she were meeting him fairly and squarely on the question they started with. Sometimes he doubted if she really knew that she was behaving insincerely, or whether, if she knew it, she could help doing it. He believed her to be a more truthful nature than himself, and it was insufferable for her to be less so, and

W. D. Howells

then accuse him of illogicality.

"I have no wish to talk," he said, smothering his rage, and taking up a page of manuscript.

"Of course," she went on, as if there had been no break in their good feeling, "I know what a goose Godolphin is, and I don't wonder you're vexed with him, but you know very well that I have nothing but the good of the play in view as a work of art, and I should say that if you couldn't keep Salome from rivalling Haxard in the interest of the spectator, you had better go back to the idea of making two plays of it. I think that the 'Second Chapter' would be a very good thing to begin with."

"Why, good heavens! you said just the contrary when we decided to drop it."

"Yes, but that was when I thought you would be able to subdue Salome."

"There never was any question of subduing Salome; it was a question of subduing Atland!"

"It's the same thing; keeping the love-business in the background."

"I give it up!" Maxwell flung down his manuscript in sign of doing so. "The whole thing is a mess, and you seem to delight in tormenting me about it. How am I to give the love-business charm, and yet keep it in the background?"

"I should think you could."

"How?"

"Well, I was afraid you would give Salome too much prominence."

"Didn't you know whether I had done so or not? You knew what I had done before Godolphin came!"

"If Godolphin thinks she is too prominent, you ought to trust his instinct."

Maxwell would not answer her. He went out, and she saw him strolling down the path to the rocks. She took the manuscript and began to read it over.

He did not come back, and when she was ready to go to supper she had to go down to the rocks for him. His angry fit seemed to have passed, but he looked abjectly sad, and her heart ached at sight of him. She said, cheerfully, "I have been reading that love-business over again, Brice, and I don't find it so far out as I was afraid it was. Salome is a little too *prononcee*, but you can easily mend that. She is a delightful character, and you have given her charm—too much charm. I don't believe there's a truer woman in the whole range of the drama. She is perfect, and that is why I think you can afford to keep her back a little in the passages with Haxard. Of course, Godolphin wants to shine there. You needn't give him her speeches, but you can put them somewhere else, in some of the scenes with Atland; it won't make any difference how much she outshines *him*, poor fellow."

He would not be entreated at once, but after letting her talk on to much the same effect for awhile, he said, "I will see what can be done with it. At present I am sick of the whole thing."

"Yes, just drop it for the present," she said. "I'm hungry, aren't you?"

"I didn't know it was time."

She was very tender with him, walking up to the hotel, and all that evening she kept him amused, so that he would not want to look at his manuscript. She used him, as a wife is apt to use her husband when he is fretted and not very well, as if he were her little boy, and she did this so sweetly that Maxwell could not resent it.

The next morning she let him go to his play again, and work all the morning. He ended about noon, and told her he had done what she wanted done to the love-business, he thought, but he would not show it to her, for he said he was tired of it, and would have to go over it with Godolphin, at any rate, when he came in the afternoon. They went to the beach, but the person with the smouldering eyes failed to appear, and in fact they did not see her again at Magnolia, and they decided that she must have been passing a few days at one of the other hotels, and gone away.

Godolphin arrived in the sunniest good-humor, as if he had never had any thought of relinquishing the play, and he professed himself delighted with the changes Maxwell had made in the love-business. He said the character of Salome had the true proportion to all the rest now; and Maxwell understood that he would not be jealous of the actress who played the part, or feel her a dangerous rival in the public favor. He approved of the transposition of the speeches that Maxwell had made, or at least he no longer openly coveted them for Haxard.

What was more important to Maxwell was that Louise seemed finally contented with the part, too, and said that now, no matter what Godolphin wanted, she would never let it be touched again. "I am glad you have got that 'impassioned' rubbish out. I never thought that was in character with Salome."

The artistic consciousness of Maxwell, which caught all the fine reluctances and all the delicate feminine preferences of his wife, was like a subtle web woven around him, and took everything, without his willing it, from within him as well as from without, and held it inexorably for future use. He knew the source of the impassioned rubbish which had displeased his wife; and he had felt while he was employing it that he was working in a commoner material than the rest of Salome's character; but he had experimented with it in the hope that she might not notice it. The fact that she had instantly noticed it, and had generalized the dislike which she only betrayed at last, after she had punished him sufficiently, remained in the meshes of the net he wore about his mind, as something of value, which he could employ to exquisite effect if he could once find a scheme fit for it.

In the meantime it would be hard to say whether Godolphin continued more a sorrow or a joy to Maxwell, who was by no means always of the same mind about him. He told his wife sometimes, when she was pitying him, that it was a good discipline for him to work with such a man, for it taught him a great deal about himself, if it did not teach him much else. He said that it tamed his overweening pride to find that there was artistic ability employing itself with literature which was so unlike literary ability. Godolphin conceived perfectly of the literary intention in the fine passages of the play, and enjoyed their beauty, but he did not value them any more than the poorest and crudest verbiage that promised him a point. In fact, Maxwell found that in two or three places the actor was making a wholly wrong version of his words, and maturing in his mind an effect from his error that he was rather loath to give up, though when he was instructed as to their true meaning, he saw how he could get a better effect out of it. He had an excellent intelligence, but this was employed so entirely in the study of impression that significance was often a secondary matter with him. He had not much humor, and Maxwell doubted if he felt it much in others, but he told a funny story admirably, and did character-stuff, as he called it, with the subtlest sense; he had begun in sketches of the variety type. Sometimes Maxwell thought him very well versed in the history and theory of the drama; but there were other times when his ignorance seemed almost creative in that direction. He had apparently no feeling for values; he would want a good effect used, without regard to the havoc it made of the whole picture, though doubtless if it could have been realized to him, he would have abhorred it as thoroughly as Maxwell himself. He would come over from Manchester one day with a notion for the play so bad that it almost made Maxwell shed tears; and the next with something so good that Maxwell marvelled at it; but Godolphin seemed to value the one no more than the other. He was a creature of moods the most extreme; his faith in Maxwell was as profound as his abysmal distrust of him; and his frank and open nature was full of suspicion. He was like a child in the simplicity of his selfishness, as far as his art was concerned, but in all matters aside from it he was chaotically generous. His formlessness was sometimes almost distracting; he presented himself to the author's imagination as mere human material, waiting to be moulded in this shape or that. From day to day, from week to week, Maxwell lived in a superficial uncertainty whether Godolphin had really taken his play, or would ever produce it; yet at the bottom of his heart he confided in the promises which the actor lavished upon him in both the written and the spoken word. They had an agreement carefully drawn up as to all the business between them, but he knew that Godolphin would not be held by any clause of it that he wished to break; he did not believe that Godolphin under-stood what it bound him to, either when he signed it or afterward; but he was sure that he would do not only what was right, but what was noble, if he could be taken at the right moment. Upon the whole, he liked him; in a curious sort, he respected and honored him; and he defended him against Mrs. Maxwell when she said Godolphin was wearing her husband's life out, and that if he made the play as greatly successful as "Hamlet," or the "Trip to Chinatown," he would not be worth what it cost them both in time and temper.

They lost a good deal of time and temper with the play, which was almost a conjugal affair with them, and the struggle to keep up a show of gay leisure before the summering world up and down the coast told upon Mrs. Maxwell's nerves. She did not mind the people in the hotel so much; they were very nice, but she did not know many of them, and she could not care for them as she did for her friends who came up from Beverly Farms and over from Manchester. She hated to call Maxwell from his work at such times, not only because she pitied him, but because he came to help her receive her friends with such an air of gloomy absence and open reluctance; and she had hated still worse to say he was busy with his play, the play he was writing for Mr. Godolphin. Her friends were apparently unable to imagine anyone writing a play so seriously, and they were unable to imagine Mr. Godolphin at all, for they had never heard of him; the splendor of his unknown name took them more than anything else. As for getting Maxwell to return their visits with her, when men had come with the ladies who called upon her, she could only manage it if he was so fagged with working at his play that he was too weak to resist her will, and even then he had to be torn from it almost by main force. He behaved so badly in the discharge of some of these duties to society, and was, to her eye at least, so bored and worried by them that she found it hard to forgive him, and made him suffer for it on the way home till she relented at the sight of his thin face, the face that she loved, that she had thought the world well lost for. After the third or fourth time she made him go with her she gave it up and went alone, though she was aware that it might look as if they were not on good terms. She only obliged him after that to go with her to her father's, where she would not allow any shadow of suspicion to fall upon their happiness, and where his absent-mindedness would be accounted for. Her mother seemed to understand it better than her father, who, she could see, sometimes inwardly resented it as neglect. She also exacted of Maxwell that he should not sit silent through a whole meal at the hotel, and that, if he did not or could not talk, he should keep looking at her, and smiling and nodding, now and then. If he would remember to do this she would do all the talking herself. Sometimes he did not remember, and then she trod on his foot in vain.

The droll side of the case often presented itself for her relief, and, after all, she knew beforehand that this was the manner of man she was marrying, and she was glad to marry him. She was happier than she had ever dreamed of being. She was one of those women who live so largely in their sympathies that if these were employed she had no thought of herself, and not to have any thought of one's self is to be blessed. Maxwell had no thought of anything but his work, and that made his bliss; if she could have no thought but of him in his work, she could feel herself in Heaven with him.

VII

July and August went by, and it was time for Godolphin to take the road again. By this time Maxwell's play was in as perfect form as it could be until it was tried upon the stage and then overhauled for repairs. Godolphin had decided to try it first in Toronto, where he was going to open, and then to give it in the West as often as he could. If it did as well as he expected he would bring it on for a run in New York about the middle of December. He would want Maxwell at the rehearsals there, but for the present he said he preferred to stage-manage it himself; they had talked it up so fully that he had all the author's intentions in mind.

He came over from Manchester the day before his vacation ended to take leave of the Maxwells. He was in great spirits with the play, but he confessed to a misgiving in regard to the lady whom he had secured for the part of Salome. He said there was only one woman he ever saw fit to do that part, but when he named the actress the Maxwells had to say they had never heard of her before. "She is a Southerner. She is very well known in the West," Godolphin said.

Louise asked if she had ever played in Boston, and when he said she had not, Louise said "Oh!"

Maxwell trembled, but Godolphin seemed to find nothing

W. D. Howells

latent in his wife's offensive tone, and after a little further talk they all parted on the friendliest terms. The Maxwells did not hear from him for a fortnight, though he was to have tried the play in Toronto at least a week earlier. Then there came a telegram from Midland:

> "*Tried play here last night. Went like wildfire. Will write.*"
>
> GODOLPHIN.

The message meant success, and the Maxwells walked the air. The production of the piece was mentioned in the Associated Press despatches to the Boston papers, and though Mrs. Maxwell studied these in vain for some verbal corroboration of Godolphin's jubilant message, she did not lose faith in it, nor allow her husband to do so. In fact, while they waited for Godolphin's promised letter, they made use of their leisure to count the chickens which had begun to hatch. The actor had agreed to pay the author at the rate of five dollars an act for each performance of the play, and as it was five acts long a simple feat of arithmetic showed that the nightly gain from it would be twenty-five dollars, and that if it ran every night and two afternoons, for matinees, the weekly return from it would be two hundred dollars. Besides this, Godolphin had once said, in a moment of high content with the piece, that if it went as he expected it to go he would pay Maxwell over and above this twenty-five dollars a performance five per cent. of the net receipts whenever these passed one thousand dollars. His promise had not been put in writing, and Maxwell had said at the time that he should be satisfied with his five dollars an act, but he had told his wife of it, and they had both agreed that Godolphin would keep it. They now took it into the account in summing up their gains, and Mrs. Maxwell thought it reasonable to figure at least twenty-five dollars more from it for each time the play was given; but as this brought the weekly sum up to four hundred dollars, she so far yielded to her husband as to scale the total at three hundred dollars, though she said it was absurd to put it at any such figure. She refused, at any rate, to estimate their earnings from the season at less than fifteen thousand dollars. It was useless for Maxwell to urge that Godolphin had other pieces in his repertory, things that had made his reputation, and that he would naturally want to give sometimes. She asked him whether Godolphin himself had not voluntarily said that if the piece went as he expected he would play nothing else as long as he lived, like Jefferson with Rip Van Winkle; and here, she said, it had already, by his own showing, gone at once like wildfire. When Maxwell pleaded that they did not know what wildfire meant she declared that it meant an overwhelming house and unbridled rapture in the audience; it meant an instant and lasting triumph for the play. She began to praise Godolphin, or, at least, to own herself mistaken in some of her decrials of him. She could not be kept from bubbling over to two or three ladies at the hotel, where it was quickly known what an immense success the first performance of Maxwell's play had been. He was put to shame by several asking him when they were to have it in Boston, but his wife had no embarrassment in answering that it would probably be kept the whole winter in New York, and not come to Boston till some time in the early spring.

She was resolved, now, that he should drive over to Beverly Farms with her, and tell her father and mother about the success of the play. She had instantly telegraphed them on getting Godolphin's despatch, and she began to call out to her father as soon as she got inside the house, and saw him coming down the stairs in the hall, "*Now*, what do you say, papa? Isn't it glorious? Didn't I tell you it would be the greatest success? Did you ever hear anything like it? Where's mamma? If she shouldn't be at home, I don't know what I shall do!"

"She's here," said her father, arriving at the foot of the stairs, where Louise embraced him, and then let him shake hands with her husband. "She's dressing. We were just going over to see you."

"Well, you've been pretty deliberate about it! Here it's after lunch, and I telegraphed you at ten o'clock." She went on to bully her father more and more, and to flourish Maxwell's triumph in his face. "We're going to have three hundred dollars a week from it at the very least, and fifteen thousand dollars for the season. What do you think of that? Isn't that pretty good, for two people that had nothing in the world yesterday? What do you say *now*, papa?"

There were all sorts of lurking taunts, demands, reproaches, in these words, which both the men felt, but they smiled across her, and made as if they were superior to her simple exultation.

"I should say you had written the play yourself, Louise," said her father.

"No," answered her husband, "Godolphin wrote the play; or I've no doubt he's telling the reporters so by this time."

Louise would not mind them. "Well, I don't care! I want papa to acknowledge that I was right, for once. Anybody could believe in Brice's genius, but I believed in his star, and I always knew that he would get on, and I was all for his giving up his newspaper work, and devoting himself to the drama; and now the way is open to him, and all he has got to do is to keep on writing."

"Come now, Louise," said her husband.

"Well," her father interposed, "I'm glad of your luck,

Maxwell. It isn't in my line, exactly, but I don't believe I could be any happier, if it were. After all, it's doing something to elevate the stage. I wish someone would take hold of the pulpit."

Maxwell shrugged. "I'm not strong enough for that, quite. And I can't say that I had any conscious intention to elevate the stage with my play."

"But you had it unconsciously, Brice," said Louise, "and it can't help having a good effect on life, too."

"It will teach people to be careful how they murder people," Maxwell assented.

"Well, it's a great chance," said Hilary, with the will to steer a middle course between Maxwell's modesty and Louise's overweening pride. "There really isn't anything that people talk about more. They discuss plays as they used to discuss sermons. If you've done a good play, you've done a good thing."

His wife hastened to make answer for him. "He's done a *great* play, and there are no ifs or ans about it." She went on to celebrate Maxwell's achievement till he was quite out of countenance, for he knew that she was doing it mainly to rub his greatness into her father, and he had so much of the old grudge left that he would not suffer himself to care whether Hilary thought him great or not. It was a relief when Mrs. Hilary came in. Louise became less defiant in her joy then, or else the effect of it was lost in Mrs. Hilary's assumption of an entire expectedness in the event. Her world was indeed so remote from the world of art that she could value success in it only as it related itself to her family, and it seemed altogether natural to her that her daughter's husband should take its honors. She was by no means a stupid woman; for a woman born and married to wealth, with all the advantages that go with it, she was uncommonly intelligent; but she could not help looking upon aesthetic honors of any sort as in questionable taste. She would have preferred position in a son-in-law to any distinction appreciable to the general, but wanting that it was fit he should be distinguished in the way he chose. In her feeling it went far to redeem the drama that it should be related to the Hilarys by marriage, and if she had put her feeling into words, which always oversay the feelings, they would have been to the effect that the drama had behaved very well indeed, and deserved praise. This is what Mrs. Hilary's instinct would have said, but, of course, her reason would have said something quite different, and it was her reason that spoke to Maxwell, and expressed a pleasure in his success that was very gratifying to him. He got on with her better than with Hilary, partly because she was a woman and he was a man, and partly because, though she had opposed his marriage with Louise more steadily than her husband, there had been no open offence between them. He did not easily forgive a hurt to his pride, and Hilary, with all his good will since, and his quick repentance at the time, had never made it quite right with Maxwell for treating him rudely once, when he came to him so helplessly in the line of his newspaper work. They were always civil to each other, and they would always be what is called good friends; they had even an air of mutual understanding, as regarded Louise and her exuberances. Still, she was so like her father in these, and so unlike her mother, that it is probable the understanding between Hilary and Maxwell concerning her was only the understanding of men, and that Maxwell was really more in sympathy with Mrs. Hilary, even about Louise, even about the world. He might have liked it as much as she, if he had been as much of it, and he thought so well of it as a world that he meant to conquer one of the chief places in it. In the meantime he would have been very willing to revenge himself upon it, to satirize it, to hurt it, to humble it—but for his own pleasure, not the world's good.

Hilary wanted the young people to stay the afternoon, and have dinner, but his wife perceived that they wished to be left alone in their exultation, and she would not let him keep them beyond a decent moment, or share too much in their joy. With only that telegram from Godolphin they could not be definite about anything but their future, which Louise, at least, beheld all rose color. Just what size or shape their good fortune had already taken they did not know, and could not, till they got the letter Godolphin had promised, and she was in haste to go back to Magnolia for that, though it could not arrive before the next morning at the earliest. She urged that he might have written before telegraphing, or when he came from the theatre after the play was given. She was not satisfied with the reception of her news, and she said so to Maxwell, as soon as they started home.

"What did you want?" he retorted, in a certain vexation. "They were as cordial as they could be."

"Cordial is not enough. You can't expect anything like uproar from mamma, but she took it too much as a matter of course, and I *did* suppose papa would be a little more riotous."

"If you are going to be as exacting as that with people," Maxwell returned, "you are going to disappoint yourself frightfully; and if you insist, you will make them hate you. People can't share your happiness any more than they can share your misery; it's as much as they can do to manage their own."

"But I did think my own father and mother might have entered into it a little more," she grieved. "Well, you are right, Brice, and I will try to hold in after this. It wasn't for myself I cared."

W. D. Howells

"I know," said Maxwell, so appreciatively that she felt all her loss made up to her, and shrunk closer to him in the buggy he was driving with a lax, absent-minded rein. "But I think a little less Fourth of July on my account would be better."

"Yes, you are wise, and I shall not say another word about it to anybody; just treat it as a common every-day event."

He laughed at what was so far from her possibilities, and began to tell her of the scheme for still another play that had occurred to him while they were talking with her father. She was interested in the scheme, but more interested in the involuntary workings of his genius, and she celebrated that till he had to beg her to stop, for she made him ashamed of himself even in the solitude of the woodland stretches they were passing through. Then he said, as if it were part of the same strain of thought, "You have to lose a lot of things in writing a play. Now, for instance, that beautiful green light there in the woods." He pointed to a depth of the boscage where it had almost an emerald quality, it was so vivid, so intense. "If I were writing a story about two lovers in such a light, and how it bathed their figures and illumined their faces, I could make the reader feel it just as I did. I could make them see it. But if I were putting them in a play, I should have to trust the carpenter and the scene-painter for the effect; and you know what broken reeds they are."

"Yes," she sighed, "and some day I hope you will write novels. But now you've made such a success with this play that you must do some others, and when you've got two or three going steadily you can afford to take up a novel. It would be wicked to turn your back on the opportunity you've won."

He silently assented and said, "I shall be all the the better novelist for waiting a year or two."

VIII

There was no letter from Godolphin in the morning, but in the course of the forenoon there came a newspaper addressed in his handwriting, and later several others. They were Midland papers, and they had each, heavily outlined in ink, a notice of the appearance of Mr. Launcelot Godolphin in a new play written expressly for him by a young Boston *litterateur*. Mr. Godolphin believed the author to be destined to make his mark high in the dramatic world, he said in the course of a long interview in the paper which came first, an evening edition preceeding the production of the piece, and plainly meant to give the public the right perspective. He had entered into a generous expression of his own feelings concerning it, and had given Maxwell full credit for the lofty conception of an American drama, modern in spirit, and broad in purpose. He modestly reserved to himself such praise as might be due for the hints his life-long knowledge of the stage had enabled him to offer the dramatist. He told how they had spent the summer near each other on the north shore of Massachusetts, and had met almost daily; and the reporter got a picturesque bit out of their first meeting at the actor's hotel, in Boston, the winter before, when the dramatist came to lay the scheme of the play before Godolphin, and Godolphin made up his mind before he had heard him half through, that he should want the piece. He had permitted himself a personal sketch of Maxwell, which lost none of its original advantages in the diction of the reporter, and which represented him as young, slight in figure, with a refined and delicate face, bearing the stamp of intellectual force; a journalist from the time he left school, and one of the best exponents of the formative influences of the press in the training of its votaries. From time to time it was hard for Maxwell to make out whose words the interview was couched in, but he acquitted Godolphin of the worst, and he certainly did not accuse him of the flowery terms giving his patriotic reasons for not producing the piece first in Toronto as he had meant to do. It appeared that, upon second thoughts, he had reserved this purely American drama for the opening night of his engagement in one of the most distinctively American cities, after having had it in daily rehearsal ever since the season began.

"I should think they had Pinney out there," said Maxwell, as he and his wife looked over the interview, with their cheeks together.

"Not at all!" she retorted. "It isn't the least like Pinney," and he was amazed to find that she really liked the stuff. She said that she was glad, now, that she understood why Godolphin had not opened with the play in Toronto, as he had promised, and she thoroughly agreed with him that it ought first to be given on our own soil. She was dashed for a moment when Maxwell made her reflect that they were probably the losers of four or five hundred dollars by the delay; then she said she did not care, that it was worth the money. She did not find the personal account of Maxwell offensive, though she contended that it did not do him full justice, and she cut out the interview and pasted it in a book, where she was going to keep all the notices of his play and every printed fact concerning it. He told her she would have to help herself out with some of the fables, if she expected to fill her book, and she said she did not care for that, either, and probably it was just such things as this interview that drew attention to the play, and must have made it go like wildfire that first night in Midland. Maxwell owned that it was but too likely, and then he waited hungrily for further word of his play, while she expected the next mail in cheerful faith.

It brought them four or five morning papers, and it seemed from these that a play might have gone like wildfire, and yet not been seen by a very large number of people. The papers agreed in a sense of the graceful compliment paid their city by Mr. Godolphin, who was always a favorite there, in producing his new piece at one of their theatres, and confiding it at once to the judgment of a cultivated audience, instead of trying it first in a subordinate place, and bringing it on with a factitious reputation worked up from all sorts of unknown sources. They agreed, too, that his acting had never been better; that it had great smoothness, and that it rose at times into passion, and was full of his peculiar force. His company was well chosen, and his support had an even excellence which reflected great credit upon the young star, who might be supposed, if he had followed an unwise tradition, to be willing to shine at the expense of his surroundings. His rendition of the role of Haxard was magnificent in one journal, grand in another, superb in a third, rich, full and satisfying in a fourth, subtle and conscientious in a fifth. Beyond this, the critics ceased to be so much of one mind. They were, by a casting vote, adverse to the leading lady, whom the majority decided an inadequate Salome, without those great qualities which the author had evidently meant to redeem a certain coquettish lightness in her; the minority held that she had grasped the role with intelligence, and expressed with artistic force a very refined intention in it. The minority hinted that Salome was really the great part in the piece, and that in her womanly endeavor to win back the lover whom she had not at first prized at his true worth, while her heart was wrung by sympathy with her unhappy

W. D. Howells

father in the mystery brooding over him, she was a far more interesting figure than the less complex Haxard; and they intimated that Godolphin had an easier task in his portrayal. They all touched more or less upon the conduct of the subordinate actors in their parts, and the Maxwells, in every case, had to wade through their opinions of the playing before they got to their opinions of the play, which was the only vital matter concerned.

Louise would have liked to read them, as she had read the first, with her arm across Maxwell's shoulder, and, as it were, with the same eye and the same mind, but Maxwell betrayed an uneasiness under the experiment which made her ask: "Don't you *like* to have me put my arm round you, Brice?"

"Yes, yes," he answered, impatiently, "I like to have you put your arm around me on all proper occasions; but—it isn't favorable to collected thought."

"Why, *I* think it is," she protested with pathos, and a burlesque of her pathos. "I never think half so well as when I have my arm around you. Then it seems as if I thought with your mind. I feel so judicial."

"Perhaps I feel too emotional, under the same conditions, and think with *your* mind. At any rate, I can't stand it; and we can't both sit in the same chair either. Now, you take one of the papers and go round to the other side of the table. I want to have all my faculties for the appreciation of this noble criticism; it's going to be full of instruction."

He made her laugh, and she feigned a pout in obeying him; but, nevertheless, in her heart she felt herself postponed to the interest that was always first in him, and always before his love.

"And don't talk," he urged, "or keep calling out, or reading passages ahead. I want to get all the sense there doesn't seem to be in this thing."

In fact the critics had found themselves confronted with a task which is always confusing to criticism, in the necessity of valuing a work of art so novel in material that it seems to refuse the application of criterions. As he followed their struggles in the endeavor to judge his work by such canons of art as were known to them, instead of taking it frankly upon the plane of nature and of truth, where he had tried to put it, and blaming or praising him as he had failed or succeeded in this, he was more and more bowed down within himself before the generous courage of Godolphin in rising to an appreciation of his intention. He now perceived that he was a man of far more uncommon intelligence than he had imagined him, and that in taking his play Godolphin had shown a zeal for the drama which was not likely to find a response in criticism, whatever its fate with the public might be. The critics frankly owned that in spite of its defects the piece had a cordial reception from the audience; that the principal actors were recalled again and again, and they reported that Godolphin had spoken both for the author and himself in acknowledging the applause, and had disclaimed all credit for their joint success. This made Maxwell ashamed of the suspicion he had harbored that Godolphin would give the impression of a joint authorship, at the least. He felt that he had judged the man narrowly and inadequately, and he decided that as soon as he heard from him, he would write and make due reparation for the tacit wrong he had done him.

Upon the whole he had some reason to be content with the first fortune of his work, whatever its final fate might be. To be sure, if the audience which received it was enthusiastic, it was confessedly small, and it had got no more than a

W. D. Howells

foothold in the public favor. It must remain for further trial to prove it a failure or a success. His eye wandered to the column of advertised amusements for the pleasure of seeing the play announced there for the rest of the week. There was a full list of the pieces for the time of Godolphin's stay; but it seemed that neither at night nor at morning was Maxwell's play to be repeated. The paper dropped from his hand.

"What is the matter?" his wife asked, looking up from her own paper. "This poor man is the greatest possible goose. He doesn't seem to know what he is talking about, even when he praises you. But of course he has to write merely from a first impression. Do you want to change papers?"

Maxwell mechanically picked his up, and gave it to her. "The worst of it is," he said, with the sardonic smile he had left over from an unhappier time of life, "that he won't have an opportunity to revise his first impression."

"What do you mean?"

He told her, but she could not believe him till she had verified the fact by looking at the advertisements in all the papers.

Then she asked: "What in the world *does* he mean?"

"Not to give it there any more, apparently. He hasn't entered upon the perpetual performance of the piece. But if he isn't like Jefferson, perhaps he's like Rip; he don't count this time. Well, I might have known it! Why did I ever trust one of that race?" He began to walk up and down the room, and to fling out, one after another, the expressions of his scorn and his self-scorn. "They have no idea of what good faith is, except as something that brings down the house when they register a noble vow. But I don't blame him; I blame myself. What an ass, what an idiot, I was! Why, *he* could have told me not to believe in his promises; he is a perfectly honest man, and would have done it, if I had appealed to him. He didn't expect me to believe in them, and from the wary way I talked, I don't suppose he thought I did. He hadn't the measure of my folly; I hadn't, myself!"

"Now, Brice!" his wife called out to him, severely, "I won't have you going on in that way. When I denounced Godolphin you wouldn't listen to me; and when I begged and besought you to give him up, you always said he was the only man in the world for you, till I got to believing it, and I believe it now. Why, dearest," she added, in a softer tone, "don't you see that he probably had his programme arranged all beforehand, and couldn't change it, just because your play happened to be a hit? I'm sure he paid you a great compliment by giving it the first night. Now, you must just wait till you hear from him, and you may be sure he will have a good reason for not repeating it there."

"Oh, Godolphin would never lack for a good reason. And I can tell you what his reason in this case will be: that the thing was practically a failure, and that he would have lost money if he had kept it on."

"Is that what is worrying you? I don't believe it was a failure. I think from all that the papers say, and the worst that they say, the piece was a distinct success. It was a great success with nice people, you can see that for yourself, and it will be a popular success, too; I know it will, as soon as it gets a chance. But you may be sure that Godolphin has some scheme about it, and that if he doesn't give it again in Midland, it's because he wants to make people curious about it, and hold it in reserve, or something like that. At any rate, I think you ought to wait for his letter before you denounce him."

Maxwell laughed again at these specious arguments, but he could not refuse to be comforted by them, and he had really nothing to do but to wait for Godolphin's letter. It did not come the next mail, and then his wife and he collated his dispatch with the newspaper notices, and tried to make up a judicial opinion from their combined testimony concerning the fate of the play with the audience. Their scrutiny of the telegram developed the fact that it must have been sent the night of the performance, and while Godolphin was still warm from his recalls and from the congratulations of his friends; it could not have reached them so soon as it did in the morning if it had been sent to the office then; it was not a night message, but it had probably lain in the office over night. In this view it was not such valuable testimony to the success of the play as it had seemed before. But a second and a third reading of the notices made them seem friendlier than at first. The Maxwells now perceived that they had first read them in the fever of their joy from Godolphin's telegram, and that their tempered approval had struck cold upon them because they were so overheated. They were really very favorable, after all, and they witnessed to an interest in the play which could not be ignored. Very likely the interest in it was partly from the fact that Godolphin had given it, but apart from this it was evident that the play had established a claim of its own. The mail, which did not bring a letter from Godolphin, brought another copy of that evening paper which had printed the anticipatory interview with him, and this had a long and careful consideration of the play in its editorial columns, apparently written by a lover of the drama, as well as a lover of the theatre. Very little regard was paid to the performance, but a great deal to the play, which was skilfully analyzed, and praised and blamed in the right places. The writer did not attempt to forecast its fate, but he said that whatever its fate with the public might be, here, at least, was a step in the direction of the drama dealing with facts of American life—simply, vigorously, and honestly. It had faults of construction, but the faults were not the faults of weakness. They were rather the effects of a young talent addressing itself to the management of material too rich, too abundant for the scene, and allowing itself to touch the borders of melodrama in its will to enforce some tragic points of the intrigue. But it was not mawkish and it was not romantic. In its highest reaches it made you think, by its stern and unflinching fidelity to the implications, of Ibsen; but it was not too much to say that it had a charm often wanting to that master. It was full of the real American humor; it made its jokes, as Americans did, in the very face of the most disastrous possibilities; and in the love-passages it was delicious. The whole episode of the love between Haxard's daughter, Salome, and Atland was simply the sweetest and freshest bit of nature in the modern drama. It daringly portrayed a woman in circumstances where it was the convention to ignore that she ever was placed, and it lent a grace of delicate comedy to the somber ensemble of the piece, without lowering the dignity of the action or detracting from the sympathy the spectator felt for the daughter of the homicide; it rather heightened this.

Louise read the criticism aloud, and then she and Maxwell looked at each other. It took their breath away; but Louise got her breath first. "Who in the world would have dreamed that there was any one who could write such a criticism, *out there*?"

Maxwell took the paper, and ran the article over again. Then he said, "If the thing did nothing more than get itself appreciated in that way, I should feel that it had done enough. I wonder who the fellow is! Could it be a woman?"

There was, in fact, a feminine fineness in the touch, here and there, that might well suggest a woman, but they finally decided against the theory: Louise said that a woman writer would not have the honesty to own that the part Salome played in getting back her lover was true to life, though every woman who saw it would know that it was. She examined the wrapper of the newspaper, and made sure that it was addressed in Godolphin's hand, and she said that if he did not speak of the article in his letter, Maxwell must write out to the newspaper and ask who had done it.

Godolphin's letter came at last, with many excuses for his delay. He said he had expected the newspaper notices to speak for him, and he seemed to think that they had all been altogether favorable to the play. It was not very consoling to have him add that he now believed the piece would have run the whole week in Midland, if he had kept it on; but he had arranged merely to give it a trial, and Maxwell would understand how impossible it was to vary a programme which had once been made out. One thing was certain, however: the piece was an assured success, and a success of the most flattering and brilliant kind, and Godolphin would give it a permanent place in his *repertoire*. There was no talk of his playing nothing else, and there was no talk of putting the piece on for a run, when he opened in New York. He said he had sent Maxwell a paper containing a criticism in the editorial columns, which would serve to show him how great an interest the piece had excited in Midland, though he believed the article was not written by one of the regular force, but was contributed from the outside by a young fellow who had been described to Godolphin as a sort of Ibsen crank. At the close, he spoke of certain weaknesses which the piece had developed in the performance, and casually mentioned that he would revise it at these points as he found the time; it appeared to him that it needed overhauling, particularly in the love episode; there was too much of that, and the interest during an entire act centred so entirely upon Salome that, as he had foreseen, the role of Haxard suffered.

IX

The Maxwells stared at each other in dismay when they had finished this letter, which Louise had opened, but which they had read together, she looking over his shoulder. All interest in the authorship of the article of the Ibsen crank, all interest in Godolphin's apparent forgetfulness of his solemn promises to give the rest of his natural life to the performance of the piece, was lost in amaze at the fact that he was going to revise it to please himself, and to fashion Maxwell's careful work over in his own ideal of the figure he should make in it to the public. The thought of this was so petrifying that even Louise could not at once find words for it, and they were both silent, as people sometimes are, when a calamity has befallen them, in the hope that if they do not speak it will turn out a miserable dream.

"Well, Brice," she said at last, "you certainly never expected *this*!"

"No," he answered with a ghastly laugh; "this passes my most sanguine expectations, even of Godolphin. Good Heaven! Fancy the botch he will make of it!"

"You mustn't let him touch it. You must demand it back, peremptorily. You must telegraph!"

"What a mania you have for telegraphing," he retorted. "A special delivery postage-stamp will serve every purpose. He isn't likely to do the piece again for a week, at the earliest." He thought for awhile, and then he said: "In a week he'll have a chance to change his mind so often, that perhaps he won't revise and overhaul it, after all."

"But he mustn't think that you would suffer it for an instant," his wife insisted. "It's an indignity that you should not submit to; it's an outrage!"

"Very likely," Maxwell admitted, and he began to walk the floor, with his head fallen, and his fingers clutched together behind him. The sight of his mute anguish wrought upon his wife and goaded her to more and more utterance.

"It's an insult to your genius, Brice, dear, and you must resent it. I am sure I have been as humble about the whole affair as any one could be, and I should be the last person to wish you to do anything rash. I bore with Godolphin's suggestions, and I let him worry you to death with his plans for spoiling your play, but I certainly didn't dream of anything so high-handed as his undertaking to work it over himself, or I should have insisted on your breaking with him long ago. How patient you have been through it all! You've shown so much forbearance, and so much wisdom, and so much delicacy in dealing with his preposterous ideas, and then, to have it all thrown away! It's too bad!"

Maxwell kept walking hack and forth, and Louise began again at a new point.

"I was willing to have it remain simply a *succes d'estime*, as far as Midland was concerned, though I think you were treated abominably in that, for he certainly gave you reason to suppose that he would do it every night there. He says himself that it would have run the whole week; and you can see from that article how it was growing in public favor all the time. What has become of his promise to play nothing else, I should like to know? And he's only played it once, and now he proposes to revise it himself!"

Still Maxwell walked on and she continued:

"I don't know what I shall say to my family. They can never understand such a thing, never! Papa couldn't conceive of giving a promise and not keeping it, much less giving a promise just for the *pleasure* of breaking it. What shall I tell them, Brice? I can't bear to say that Godolphin is going to make your play over, unless I can say at the same time that you've absolutely forbidden him to do so. That's why I wanted you to telegraph. I wanted to say you had telegraphed."

Maxwell stopped in his walk and gazed at her, but she could feel that he did not see her, and she said:

"I don't know that it's actually necessary for me to say anything at present. I can show them the notices, or that article alone. It's worth all the rest put together, and then we can wait, and see if we hear anything more from Godolphin. But now I don't want you to lose any more time. You must write to him at once, and absolutely forbid him to touch your play. Will you?"

Her husband returned from his wanderings of mind and body, and as he dropped upon the lounge at her side, he said, gently, "No, I don't think I'll write at all, Louise."

"Not write at all! Then you're going to let him tamper with that beautiful work of yours?"

"I'm going to wait till I hear from him again. Godolphin is a good fellow—"

"Oh!"

"And he won't be guilty of doing me injustice. Besides," and here Maxwell broke off with a laugh that had some gayety in it, "he couldn't. Godolphin is a fine actor, and he's going to be a great one, but his gifts are not in the line of literature."

"I should think not!"

"He couldn't change the piece any more than if he couldn't read or write. And if he could, when it came to touching it, I don't believe he would, because the fact would remind him that it wasn't fair. He has to realize things in the objective way before he can realize them at all. That's the stage. If they can have an operator climbing a real telegraph-pole to tap the wire and telegraph the girl he loves that he is dead, so that she can marry his rich rival and go to Europe and cultivate her gift for sculpture, they feel that they have got real life."

Louise would not be amused, or laugh with her husband at this. "Then what in the world does Godolphin mean?" she demanded.

"Why, being interpreted out of actor's parlance, he means that he wishes he could talk the play over with me again and be persuaded that he is wrong about it."

"I must say," Louise remarked, after a moment for mastering the philosophy of this, "that you take it very strangely, Brice."

"I've thought it out," said Maxwell.

"And what are you going to do?"

"I am going to wait the turn of events. My faith in Godolphin is unshaken—such as it is."

"And what is going to be our attitude in regard to it?"

"Attitude? With whom?"

"With our friends. Suppose they ask us about the play, and how it is getting along. And my family?"

"I don't think it will be necessary to take any attitude. They can think what they like. Let them wait the turn of events, too. If we can stand it, they can."

"No, Brice," said his wife. "That won't do. We might be silently patient ourselves, but if we left them to believe that it was all going well, we should be living a lie."

"What an extraordinary idea!"

"I've told papa and mamma—we've both told them, though I did the talking, you can say—that the play was a splendid success, and Godolphin was going to give it seven or eight times a week; and now if it's a failure—"

"It *isn't* a failure!" Maxwell retorted, as if hurt by the notion.

"No matter! If he's only going to play it once a fortnight or so, and is going to tinker it up to suit himself without saying by-your-leave to you, I say we're occupying a false position, and that's what I mean by living a lie."

Maxwell looked at her in that bewilderment which he was beginning to feel at the contradictions of her character. She sometimes told outright little fibs which astonished him; society fibs she did not mind at all; but when it came to people's erroneously inferring this or that from her actions, she had a yearning for the explicit truth that nothing else could appease. He, on the contrary, was indifferent to what people thought, if he had not openly misled them. Let them think this, or let them think that; it was altogether their affair, and he did not hold himself responsible; but he was ill at ease with any conventional lie on his conscience. He hated to have his wife say to people, as he sometimes overheard her saying, that he was out, when she knew he had run upstairs with his writing to escape them; she contended that it was no harm, since it deceived nobody.

Now he said, "Aren't you rather unnecessarily complex?"

"No, I'm not. And I shall tell papa as soon as I see him just how the case stands. Why, it would be dreadful if we let him believe it was all going well, and perhaps tell others that it was, and we knew all the time that it wasn't. He would hate that, and he wouldn't like us for letting him."

"Hadn't you better give the thing a chance to go right? There hasn't been time yet."

"No, dearest, I feel that since I've bragged so to papa, I ought to eat humble-pie before him as soon as possible."

"Yes. Why should you make me eat it, too?"

"I can't help that; I would if I could. But, unfortunately, we are one."

"And you seem to be the one. Suppose I should ask you not to eat humble-pie before your father?"

"Then, of course, I should do as you asked. But I hope you won't."

Maxwell did not say anything, and she went on, tenderly, entreatingly, "And I hope you'll never allow me to deceive myself about anything you do. I should resent it a great deal more than if you had positively deceived me. Will you promise me, if anything sad or bad happens, that you don't want me to know because it will make me unhappy or disagreeable, you'll tell me at once?"

"It won't be necessary. You'll find it out."

"No, do be serious, dearest. *I* am *very* serious. Will you?"

"What is the use of asking such a thing as that? It seems to me that I've invited you to a full share of the shame and sorrow that Godolphin has brought upon me."

"Yes, you have," said Louise, thoughtfully. "And you may be sure that I appreciate it. Don't you like to have me share it?"

"Well, I don't know. I might like to get at it first myself."

"Ah, you didn't like my opening Godolphin's letter when it came!"

"I shouldn't mind, now, if you would answer it."

"I shall be only too glad to answer it, if you will let me answer it as it deserves."

"That needs reflection."

X

The weather grew rough early in September, and all at once, all in a moment, as it were, the pretty watering-place lost its air of summer gayety. The sky had an inner gray in its blue; the sea looked cold. A few hardy bathers braved it out on select days in the surf, but they were purple and red when they ran up to the bath-houses, and they came out wrinkled, and hurried to their hotels, where there began to be a smell of steam-heat and a snapping of radiators in the halls. The barges went away laden to the stations, and came back empty, except at night, when they brought over the few and fewer husbands whose wives were staying down simply because they hated to go up and begin the social life of the winter. The people who had thronged the grassy-bordered paths of the village dwindled in number; the riding and driving on the roads was less and less; the native life showed itself more in the sparsity of the sojourners. The sweet fern in the open fields, and the brakes and blackberry-vines among the bowlders, were blighted with the cold wind; even the sea-weed swaying at the foot of the rocks seemed to feel a sharper chill than that of the brine. A storm came, and strewed the beach with kelp, and blew over half the bath-houses; and then the hardiest lingerer ceased to talk of staying through October. There began to be rumors at the Maxwells' hotel that it would close before the month was out; some ladies pressed the landlord for the truth, and he confessed that he expected to shut the house by the 25th. This spread dismay; but certain of the boarders said they would go to the other hotels, which were to keep open till October. The dependent cottages had been mostly emptied before; those who remained in them, if they did not go away, came into the hotel. The Maxwells themselves did this at last, for the sake of the warmth and the human companionship around the blazing hearth-fires in the parlors. They got a room with a stove in it, so that he could write; and there was a pensive, fleeting coziness in it all, with the shrinking numbers in the vast dining-room grouped at two or three tables for dinner, and then gathered in the light of the evening lamps over the evening papers. In these conditions there came, if not friendship, an intensification of acquaintance, such as is imaginable of a company of cultured castaways. Ladies who were not quite socially certain of one another in town gossiped fearlessly together; there was whist among the men; more than once it happened that a young girl played or sang by request, and not, as so often happens where a hotel is full, against the general desire. It came once to a wish that Mr. Maxwell would read something from his play; but no one had the courage to ask him. In society he was rather severe with women, and his wife was not sorry for that; she made herself all the more approachable because of it. But she discouraged the hope of anything like reading from him; she even feigned that he might not like to do it without consulting Mr. Godolphin, and if she did not live a lie concerning the status of his play, she did not scruple to tell one, now and then.

That is, she would say it was going beyond their expectations, and this was not so fabulous as it might seem, for their expectations were not so high as they had been, and Godolphin was really playing the piece once or twice a week. They heard no more from him by letter, for Maxwell had decided that it would be better not to answer his missive from Midland; but he was pretty faithful in sending the newspaper notices whenever he played, and so they knew that he had not abandoned it. They did not know whether he had carried out his threat of overhauling it; and Maxwell chose to remain in ignorance of the fact till Godolphin himself should speak again. Unless he demanded the play back he was really helpless, and he was not ready to do that, for he hoped that when the actor brought it on to New York he could talk with him about it, and come to some understanding. He had not his wife's belief in the perfection of the piece; it might very well have proved weak in places, and after his first indignation at the notion of Godolphin's revising it, he was willing to do what he could to meet his wishes. He did not so much care what shape it had in these remote theatres of the West; the real test was New York, and there it should appear only as he wished.

It was a comfort to his wife when he took this stand, and she vowed him to keep it; she would have made him go down on his knees and hold up his right hand, which was her notion of the way an oath was taken in court, but she did not think he would do it, and he might refuse to seal any vow at all if she urged it.

In the meanwhile she was not without other consolations. At her insistence he wrote to the newspaper which had printed the Ibsen crank's article on the play, and said how much pleasure it had given him, and begged his thanks to the author. They got a very pretty letter back from him, adding some praises of the piece which he said he had kept out of print because he did not want to seem too gushing about it; and he ventured some wary censures of the acting, which he said he had preferred not to criticise openly, since the drama was far more important to him than the theatre. He believed that Mr. Godolphin had a perfect conception of the part of Haxard, and a thorough respect for the piece, but his training had been altogether in the romantic school; he was working out of it, but he was not able at once to simplify himself. This was in fact the fault of the whole company. The girl who did Salome had moments of charming reality, but she too suffered from her tradition, and the rest went from bad to worse. He thought that they would all do better as they familiarized themselves with the piece, and he deeply regretted that Mr. Godolphin had been able to give it only once in Midland.

At this Mrs. Maxwell's wounds inwardly bled afresh, and she came little short of bedewing the kind letter with her tears. She made Maxwell answer it at once, and she would not let him deprecate the writer's worship of him as the first American dramatist to attempt something in the spirit of the great modern masters abroad. She contended that it would be as false to refuse this tribute as to accept one that was not due him, and there could be no doubt but it was fully and richly merited. The critic wrote again in response to Maxwell, and they exchanged three or four letters.

What was even more to Louise was the admirable behavior of her father when she went to eat humble-pie before him. He laughed at the notion of Godolphin's meddling with the play, and scolded her for not taking her husband's view of the case, which he found entirely reasonable, and the only reasonable view of it. He argued that Godolphin simply chose to assert in that way a claim to joint authorship, which he had all along probably believed he had, and he approved of Maxwell's letting him have his head in the matter, so far as the West was concerned. If he attempted to give it with any alterations of his own in the East, there would be time enough to stop him. Louise seized the occasion to confirm herself in her faith that her father admired Maxwell's genius as much as she did herself; and she tried to remember just the words he used in praising it, so that she could repeat them to Maxwell. She also committed to memory his declaration that the very fact of Godolphin's playing the piece every now and then was proof positive that he would be very reluctant to part with it, if it came to that. This seemed to her very important, and she could hardly put up with Maxwell's sardonic doubt of it.

Before they left Magnolia there came a letter from Godolphin himself, wholly different in tone from his earlier letter. He said nothing now of overhauling the piece, which he felt was gradually making its way. He was playing it at various one-night stands in the Northwest, preparatory to bringing it to Chicago and putting it on for a week, and he asked if Maxwell could not come out and see it there. He believed they were all gradually getting down to it, and the author's presence at the rehearsals would be invaluable. He felt more and more that they had a fortune in it, and it only needed careful working to realize a bonanza. He renewed his promises, in view of his success so far, to play it exclusively if the triumph could be clinched by a week's run in such a place as Chicago. He wrote from Grand Rapids, and asked Maxwell to reply to him at Oshkosh.

"Tell him you'll come, of course," said his wife.

Maxwell shook his head. "He doesn't mean this any more than he meant to revise the thing himself. He probably finds that he can't do that, and wants me to do it. But if I did it he might take it off after the first night in Chicago if the notices were unfavorable."

"But they won't be," she argued. "I *know* they won't."

"I should simply break him up from the form he's got into, if I went to the rehearsals. He must keep on doing it in his own way till he comes to New York."

"But think of the effect it will have in New York if you should happen to make it go in Chicago."

"It won't have the slightest effect. When he brings it East, it will have to make its way just as if it had never been played anywhere before."

A bright thought occurred to Louise. "Then tell him that if he will bring it on to Boston you will superintend all the rehearsals. And I will go with you to them."

Maxwell only laughed at this. "Boston wouldn't serve any better than Chicago, as far as New York is concerned. We shall have to build a success from the ground up there, if we get one. It might run a whole winter in Boston, and then we should probably begin with half a house in New York, or a third. The only advantage of trying it anywhere before, is that the actors will be warm in their parts. Besides, do you suppose Godolphin could get a theatre in Boston out of the order of his engagement there next spring?"

"Why not?"

"Simply because every night at every house is taken six months beforehand."

"Who would ever have dreamt," said Louise, ruefully, "that simply writing a play would involve any one in all these exasperating business details."

"Nobody can get free of business," Maxwell returned.

"Then I will tell you," she brightened up to say. "Why not sell him the piece outright, and wash your hands of it?"

"Because he wouldn't buy it outright, and if I washed my

hands of it he could do what he pleased with it. If he couldn't tinker it up himself he could hire some one else to do it, and that would be worse yet."

"Well, then, the only thing for us to do is to go on to New York, and wait there till Godolphin comes. I suppose papa and mamma would like to have us stay through October with them in Boston, but I don't see much sense in that, and I don't choose to have the air of living on them. I want to present an unbroken front of independence from the beginning, as far as inquiring friends are concerned; and in New York we shall be so lost to sight that nobody will know how we are living. You can work at your new play while we're waiting, and we can feel that the onset in the battle of life has sounded."

Maxwell laughed, as she meant him, at the mock heroics of her phrase, and she pulled off his hat, and rubbed his hair round on his skull in exultation at having arrived at some clear understanding. "I wouldn't have hair like silk," she jeered.

"And I wouldn't have hair like corn-silk," he returned. "At least not on my own head."

"Yes, it *is* coarse. And it's yours quite as much as mine," she said, thoughtfully. "We *do* belong to each other utterly, don't we? I never thought of it in that light before. And now our life has gone into your work, already! I can't tell you, Brice, how sweet it is to think of that love-business being our own! I shall be so proud of it on the stage! But as long as we live no one but ourselves must know anything about it. Do you suppose they will?" she asked, in sudden dismay.

He smiled. "Should you care?"

She reflected a moment. "No!" she shouted, boldly. "What difference?"

"Godolphin would pay any sum for the privilege of using the fact as an advertisement. If he could put it into Pinney's hands, and give him *carte blanche*, to work in all the romance he liked—"

"Brice!" she shrieked.

"Well, we needn't give it away, and if *we* don't, nobody else will."

"No, and we must always keep it sacredly secret. Promise me one thing!"

"Twenty!"

"That you will let me hold your hand all through the first performance of that part. Will you?"

"Why, we shall be set up like two brazen images in a box for all the first-nighters to stare at and the society reporters to describe. What would society journalism say to your holding my hand throughout the tender passages? It would be onto something personal in them in an instant."

"No; now I will show you how we will do." They were sitting in a nook of the rocks, in the pallor of the late September sunshine, with their backs against a warm bowlder. "Now give me your hand."

"Why, you've got hold of it already."

"Oh yes, so I have! Well, I'll just grasp it in mine firmly, and let them both rest on your knee, so; and fling the edge of whatever I'm wearing on my shoulders over them, or my mantle, if it's hanging on the back of the chair, so"—she flung the edge of her shawl over their clasped hands to illustrate—"and nobody will suspect the least thing. Suppose the sea was the audience—a sea of faces you know; would any one dream down there that I was squeezing your hand at all the important moments, or you squeezing mine?"

"I hope they wouldn't think me capable of doing anything so indelicate as squeezing a lady's hand," said Maxwell. "I don't know what they might think of you, though, if there was any such elaborate display of concealment as you've got up here."

"Oh, this is merely rehearsing. Of course, I shall be more adroit, more careless, when I really come to it. But what I mean is that when we first see it together, the love-business, I shall want to feel that you are feeling every instant just as I do. Will you?"

"I don't see any great objection to that. We shall both be feeling very anxious about the play, if that's what you mean."

"That's what I mean in one sense," Louise allowed. "Sha'n't you be very anxious to see how they have imagined Salome and Atland?"

"Not so anxious as about how Godolphin has 'created' Haxard."

"I care nothing about that. But if the woman who does *me* is vulgar, or underbred, or the least bit coarse, and doesn't keep the character just as sweet and delicate as you imagined it, I don't know what I shall do to her."

"Nothing violent, I hope," Maxwell suggested languidly.

"I am not so sure," said Louise. "It's a dreadfully intimate affair with me, and if I didn't like it I should hiss, anyway."

Maxwell laughed long and loud. "What a delightful thing that would be for society journalism. 'At one point the wife of the author was apparently unable to control her emotions, and she was heard to express her disapprobation by a prolonged sibilation. All eyes were turned upon the box where she sat with her husband, their hands clasped under the edge of her mantle.' No, you mustn't hiss, my dear; but if you find Salome getting too much for you you can throw a dynamite bomb at the young woman who is doing her. I dare say we shall want to blow up the whole theatre before the play is over."

"Oh, I don't believe we shall. I know the piece will go splendidly if the love-business is well done. But you can understand, can't you, just how I feel about Salome?"

"I think I can, and I am perfectly sure that you will be bitterly disappointed in her, no matter how she's done, unless you do her yourself."

"I wish I could!"

"Then the other people might be disappointed."

W. D. Howells

XI

The Maxwells went to New York early in October, and took a little furnished flat for the winter on the West Side, between two streets among the Eighties. It was in a new apartment-house, rather fine on the outside, and its balconies leaned caressingly towards the tracks of the Elevated Road, whose trains steamed back and forth under them night and day. At first they thought it rather noisy, but their young nerves were strong, and they soon ceased to take note of the uproar, even when the windows were open.

The weather was charming, as the weather of the New York October is apt to be. The month proved much milder than September had been at Magnolia. They were not very far from Central Park, and they went for whole afternoons into it. They came to have such a sense of ownership in one of the seats in the Ramble, that they felt aggrieved when they found anybody had taken it, and they resented other people's intimacy with the squirrels, which Louise always took a pocketful of nuts to feed; the squirrels got a habit of climbing into her lap for them. Sometimes Maxwell hired a boat and rowed her lazily about on the lake, while he mused and she talked. Sometimes, to be very lavish, they took places in the public carriage which plied on the drives of the Park, and went up to the tennis-grounds beyond the reservoirs, and watched the players, or the art-students sketching the autumn scenery there. They began to know, without acquaintance, certain attached or semi-attached couples; and no doubt they passed with these for lovers themselves, though they felt a vast superiority to them in virtue of their married experience; they looked upon them, though the people were sometimes their elders, as very young things, who were in the right way, but were as yet deplorably ignorant how happy they were going to be. They almost always walked back from these drives, and it was not so far but they could walk over to the North River for the sunset before their dinner, which they had late when they did that, and earlier when they did not do it. Dinner was rather a matter of caprice with them. Sometimes they dined at a French or Italian *table d'hote*; sometimes they foraged for it before they came in from their sunset, or their afternoon in the park. When dinner consisted mainly of a steak or chops, with one of the delicious salads their avenue abounded in, and some improvisation of potatoes, and coffee afterward, it was very easy to get it up in half an hour. They kept one maid, who called herself a Sweden's girl, and Louise cooked some of the things herself. She did not cook them so well as the maid, but Maxwell never knew what he was eating, and he thought it all alike good.

In their simple circumstances, Louise never missed the affluence that had flattered her whole life in her father's house. It seemed to her as if she had not lived before her marriage—as if she had always lived as she did now. She made the most of her house-keeping, but there was not a great deal of that, at the most. She knew some New York people, but it was too early yet for them to be back to town, and, besides, she doubted if she should let them know where she was; for society afflicted Maxwell, and she could not care for it unless he did. She did not wish to do anything as yet, or be anything apart from him; she was timid about going into the street without him. She wished to be always with him, and always talking to him; but it soon came to his imploring her not to talk when she was in the room where he was writing; and he often came to the table so distraught that the meal might have passed without a word but for her.

He valued her all she could possibly have desired in relation to his work, and he showed her how absolutely he rested upon her sympathy, if not her judgment, in it. He submitted everything to her, and forbore, and changed, and amended, and wrote and rewrote at her will; or when he revolted, and wrote on in defiance of her, he was apt to tear the work up. He destroyed a good deal of good literature in this way, and more than once it happened that she had tacitly changed her mind and was of his way of thinking when it was too late. In view of such a chance she made him promise that he would always show her what he had written, even when he had written wholly against her taste and wish. He was not to let his pride keep him from doing this, though, as a general thing, she took a good deal of pride in his pride, having none herself, as she believed. Whether she had or not, she was very wilful, and rather prepotent; but she never bore malice, as the phrase is, when she got the worst of anything, though she might have been quite to blame. She had in all things a high ideal of conduct, which she expected her husband to live up to when she was the prey of adverse circumstances. At other times she did her share of the common endeavor.

All through the month of October he worked at the new play, and from time to time they heard from the old play, which Godolphin was still giving, here and there, in the West. He had not made any reply to Maxwell's letter of regret that he could not come to the rehearsals at Chicago, but he sent the notices marked in the newspapers, at the various points where he played, and the Maxwells contented themselves as they could with these proofs of an unbroken amity. They expected something more direct and explicit from him when he should get to Chicago, where his engagement was to begin the first week in November. In the meantime the kind of life they were living had not that stressful unreality for Louise that it had for Maxwell on the economic side. For the first time his regular and serious habits of work did not mean the earning of money, but only the chance of earning money. Ever since he had begun the world for himself, and he had begun it very early, there had been some income from his industry; however little it was, it was certain; the salary was there for him at the end of the week when he went to the cashier's desk. His mother and he had both done so well and so wisely in their several ways of taking care of themselves, that Maxwell had not only been able to live on his earnings, but he had been able to save out of them the thousand dollars which Louise bragged of to her father, and it was this store which they were now consuming, not rapidly, indeed, but steadily, and with no immediate return in money to repair the waste. The fact kept Maxwell wakeful at night sometimes, and by day he shuddered inwardly at the shrinkage of his savings, so much swifter than their growth, though he was generously abetted by Louise in using them with frugality. She could always have had money from her father, but this was something that Maxwell would not look forward to. There could be no real anxiety for them in the situation, but for Maxwell there was care. He might be going to get a great deal out of the play he was now writing, but as yet it was in no form to show to a manager or an actor; and he might be going to get a great deal out of his old play, but so far Godolphin had made no sign that he remembered one of the most essential of the obligations which seemed all to rest so lightly upon him. Maxwell hated to remind him of it, and in the end he was very glad that he never did, or that he had not betrayed the slightest misgiving of his good faith.

One morning near the end of the month, when he was lower in his spirits than usual from this cause, there came a letter

W. D. Howells

from the editor of the Boston *Abstract* asking him if he could not write a weekly letter from New York for his old newspaper. It was a temptation, and Maxwell found it a hardship that his wife should have gone out just then to do the marketing for the day; she considered this the duty of a wife, and she fulfilled it often enough to keep her sense of it alive, but she much preferred to forage with him in the afternoon; that was poetry, she said, and the other was prose. He would have liked to talk the proposition over with her; to realize the compliment while it was fresh, to grumble at it a little, and to be supported in his notion that it would be bad business just then for him to undertake a task that might draw him away from his play too much; to do the latter well would take a great deal of time. Yet he did not feel quite that he ought to refuse it, in view of the uncertainties of the future, and it might even be useful to hold the position aside from the money it would bring him; the New York correspondent of the Boston *Abstract* might have a claim upon the attention of the managers which a wholly unaccredited playwright could not urge; there was no question of their favor with Maxwell; he would disdain to have that, even if he could get it, except by the excellence, or at least the availability of his work.

Louise did not come in until much later than usual, and then she came in looking very excited. "Well, my dear," she began to call out to him as soon as the door was opened for her, "I have seen that woman again!"

"What woman?" he asked.

"You know. That smouldering-eyed thing in the bathing-dress." She added, in answer to his stupefied gaze: "I don't mean that she was in the bathing-dress still, but her eyes were smouldering away just as they were that day on the beach at Magnolia."

"Oh!" said Maxwell, indifferently. "Where did you see her?"

"On the avenue, and I know she lives in the neighborhood somewhere, because she was shopping here on the avenue, and I could have easily followed her home if she had not taken the Elevated for down town."

"Why didn't you take it, too? It might have been a long way round, but it would have been certain. I've been wanting you here badly. Just tell me what you think of that."

He gave her the editor's letter, and she hastily ran it through. "I wouldn't think of it for a moment," she said. "Were there any letters for me?"

"It isn't a thing to be dismissed without reflection," he began.

"I thought you wanted to devote yourself entirely to the drama?"

"Of course."

"And you've always said there was nothing so killing to creative work as any sort of journalism."

"This wouldn't take more than a day or two each week, and twenty-five dollars a letter would be convenient while we are waiting for our cards to turn up."

"Oh, very well! If you are so fickle as all that, *I* don't know what to say to you." She put the letter down on the table before him, and went out of the room.

He tried to write, but with the hurt of what he felt her unkindness he could not, and after a certain time he feigned an errand into their room, where she had shut herself from

W. D. Howells

him, and found her lying down. "Are you sick?" he asked, coldly.

"Not at all," she answered. "I suppose one may lie down without being sick, as you call it. I should say ill, myself."

"I'm so glad you're not sick that I don't care what you call it."

He was going out, when she spoke again: "I didn't know you cared particularly, you are always so much taken up with your work. I suppose, if you wrote those letters for the *Abstract*, you need never think of me at all, whether I was ill or well."

"You would take care to remind me of your existence from time to time, I dare say. You haven't the habit of suffering in silence a great deal."

"You would like it better, of course, if I had."

"A great deal better, my dear. But I didn't know that you regarded my work as self-indulgence altogether. I have flattered myself now and then that I was doing it for you, too."

"Oh yes, very likely. But if you had never seen me you would be doing it all the same."

"I'm afraid so. I seem to have been made that way. I'm sorry you don't approve. I supposed you did once."

"Oh, I do approve—highly." He left her, and she heard him getting his hat and stick in the little hallway, as if he were going out of doors. She called to him, "What I wonder is how a man so self-centred that he can't look at his wife for days together, can tell whether another woman's eyes are smouldering or not."

Maxwell paused, with his hand on the knob, as if he were going to make some retort, but, perhaps because he could think of none, he went out without speaking.

He stayed away all the forenoon, walking down the river along the squalid waterside avenues; he found them in sympathy with the squalor in himself which always followed a squabble with his wife. At the end of one of the westward streets he found himself on a pier flanked by vast flotillas of canal-boats. As he passed one of these he heard the sound of furious bickering within, and while he halted a man burst from the gangway and sprang ashore, followed by the threats and curses of a woman, who put her head out of the hatch to launch them after him.

The incident turned Maxwell faint; he perceived that the case of this unhappy man, who tried to walk out of earshot with dignity, was his own in quality, if not in quantity. He felt the shame of their human identity, and he reached home with his teeth set in a hard resolve to bear and forbear in all things thereafter, rather than share ever again in misery like that, which dishonored his wife even more than it dishonored him. At the same time he was glad of a thought the whole affair suggested to him, and he wondered whether he could get a play out of it. This was the notion of showing the evil eventuation of good. Their tiffs came out of their love for each other, and no other quarrels could have the bitterness that these got from the very innermost sweetness of life. It would be hard to show this dramatically, but if it could be done the success would be worth all the toil it would cost.

At his door he realized with a pang that he could not submit the notion to his wife now, and perhaps never. But the door was pulled open before he could turn his latch-key in the

W. D. Howells

lock, and Louise threw her arms round his neck.

"Oh, dearest, guess!" she commanded between her kisses.

"Guess what?" he asked, walking her into the parlor with his arms round her. She kept her hands behind her when he released her, and they stood confronted.

"What should you consider the best news—or not news exactly; the best thing—in the world?"

"Why, I don't know. Has the play been a great success in Chicago?"

"Better than that!" she shouted, and she brought an open letter from behind her, and flourished it before him, while she went on breathlessly: "It's from Godolphin, and of course I opened it at once, for I thought if there was anything worrying in it, I had better find it out while you were gone, and prepare you for it. He's sent you a check for $300— twelve performances of the play—and he's written you the sweetest letter in the world, and I take back everything I ever said against him! Here, shall I read it? Or, no, you'll want to read it yourself. Now, sit down at your desk, and I'll put it before you, with the check on top!"

She pushed him into his chair, and he obediently read the check first, and then took up the letter. It was dated at Chicago, and was written with a certain histrionic conscious-ness, as if Godolphin enjoyed the pose of a rising young actor paying over to the author his share of the profits of their joint enterprise in their play. There was a list of the dates and places of the performances, which Maxwell noted were chiefly matinees; and he argued a distrust of the piece from this fact, which Godolphin did not otherwise betray. He said that the play constantly grew upon him, and that with such revision as they should be able to give it together when he reached New York, they would have one of the greatest plays of the modern stage. He had found that wherever he gave it the better part of his audience was best pleased with it, and he felt sure that when he put it on for a run the houses would grow up to it in every way. He was going to test it for a week in Chicago; there was no reference to his wish that Maxwell should have been present at the rehearsals there; but otherwise Godolphin's letter was as candid as it was cordial.

Maxwell read it with a silent joy which seemed to please his wife as well as if he had joined her in rioting over it. She had kept the lunch warm for him, and now she brought it in from the kitchen herself and set it before him, talking all the time.

"Well, now we can regard it as an accomplished fact, and I shall not allow you to feel any anxiety about it from this time forward. I consider that Godolphin has done his whole duty by it. He has kept the spirit of his promises if he hasn't the letter, and from this time forward I am going to trust him implicitly, and I'm going to make you. No more question of Godolphin in *this* family! Don't you long to know how it goes in Chicago? But I don't really care, for, as you say, that won't have the slightest influence in New York; and I know it will go here, anyway. Yes, I consider it, from this time on, an assured success. And isn't it delightful that, as Godolphin says, it's such a favorite with refined people?" She went on a good while to this effect, but when she had talked herself out, Maxwell had still said so little that she asked, "What is it, Brice?"

"Do you think we deserve it?" he returned, seriously.

"For squabbling so? Why, I suppose I was tired and over-wrought, or I shouldn't have done it."

"And I hadn't even that excuse," said Maxwell.

"Oh, yes you had," she retorted. "I provoked you. And if any one was to blame, I was. Do you mind it so much?"

"Yes, it tears my heart. And it makes me feel so low and mean."

"Oh, how good you are!" she began, but he stopped her.

"Don't! I'm not good; and I don't deserve success. I don't feel as if this belonged to me. I ought to send Godolphin's check back, in common honesty, common decency." He told of the quarrel he had witnessed on the canal-boat, and she loved him for his simple-hearted humility; but she said there was nothing parallel in the cases, and she would not let him think so; that it was morbid, and showed he had been overworking.

"And now," she went on, "you must write to Mr. Ricker at once and thank him, and tell him you can't do the letters for him. Will you?"

"I'll see."

"You must. I want you to reserve your whole strength for the drama. That's your true vocation, and it would be a sin for you to turn to the right or left." He continued silent, and she went on: "Are you still thinking about our scrap this morning? Well, then, I'll promise never to begin it again. Will that do?"

"Oh, I don't know that you began it. And I wasn't thinking—I was thinking of an idea for a play—the eventuation of good in evil—love evolving in hate."

"That will be grand, if you can work it out. And now you

see, don't you, that there is some use in squabbling, even?"

"I suppose nothing is lost," said Maxwell. He took out his pocket-book, and folded Godolphin's check into it.

XII

A week later there came another letter from Godolphin. It was very civil, and in its general text it did not bear out the promise of severity in its change of address to *Dear Sir*, from the *Dear Mr. Maxwell* of the earlier date.

It conveyed, in as kindly terms as could have been asked, a fact which no terms could have flattered into acceptability.

Godolphin wrote, after trying the play two nights and a matinee in Chicago, to tell the author that he had withdrawn it because its failure had not been a failure in the usual sense but had been a grievous collapse, which left him no hopes that it would revive in the public favor if it were kept on. Maxwell would be able to judge, he said, from the newspapers he sent, of the view the critics had taken of the piece; but this would not have mattered at all if it had not been the view of the public, too. He said he would not pain Maxwell by repeating the opinions which he had borne the brunt of alone; but they were such as to satisfy him fully and finally that he had been mistaken in supposing there was a part for him in the piece. He begged to return it to *Maxwell*, and he ventured to send his prompt-book with the original manuscript, which might facilitate his getting the play into other hands.

The parcel was brought in by express while they were sitting in the dismay caused by the letter, and took from them the hope that Godolphin might have written from a mood and changed his mind before sending back the piece. Neither of them had the nerve to open the parcel, which lay upon Maxwell's desk, very much sealed and tied and labelled, diffusing a faint smell of horses, as express packages mostly do, through the room.

Maxwell found strength, if not heart, to speak first. "I suppose I am to blame for not going to Chicago for the rehearsals." Louise said she did not see what that could have done to keep the play from failing, and he answered that it might have kept Godolphin from losing courage. "You see, he says he had to take the brunt of public opinion *alone*. He was sore about that."

"Oh, well, if he is so weak as that, and would have had to be bolstered up all along, you are well rid of him."

"I am certainly rid of him," Maxwell partially assented, and they both lapsed into silence again. Even Louise could not talk. They were as if stunned by the blow that had fallen on them, as all such blows fall, when it was least expected, and it seemed to the victims as if they were least able to bear it. In fact, it was a cruel reverse from the happiness they had enjoyed since Godolphin's check came, and although Maxwell had said that they must not count upon anything from him, except from hour to hour, his words conveyed a doubt that he felt no more than Louise. Now his gloomy wisdom was justified by a perfidy which she could paint in no colors that seemed black enough. Perhaps the want of these was what kept her mute at first; even when she began to talk she could only express her disdain by urging her husband to send back Godolphin's check to him. "We want nothing more to do with such a man. If he felt no obligation

W. D. Howells

to keep faith with you, it's the same as if he had sent that money out of charity."

"Yes, I have thought of that," said Maxwell. "But I guess I shall keep the money. He may regard the whole transaction as child's play; but I don't, and I never did. I worked very hard on the piece, and at the rates for space-work, merely, I earned his money and a great deal more. If I can ever do anything with it, I shall be only too glad to give him his three hundred dollars again."

She could see that he had already gathered spirit for new endeavor with the play, and her heart yearned upon him in pride and fondness. "Oh, you dear! What do you intend to do next?"

"I shall try the managers."

"Brice!" she cried in utter admiration.

He rose and said, as he took up the express package, and gave Godolphin's letter a contemptuous push with his hand, "You can gather up this spilt milk. Put it away somewhere; I don't want to see it or think of it again." He cut open the package, and found the prompt-book, which he laid aside, while he looked to see if his own copy of the play were all there.

"You are going to begin at once?" gasped Louise.

"This instant," he said. "It will be slow enough work at the best, and we mustn't lose time. I shall probably have to go the rounds of all the managers, but I am not going to stop till I have gone the rounds. I shall begin with the highest, and I sha'n't stop till I reach the lowest."

"But when? How? You haven't thought it out."

"Yes, I have. I have been thinking it out ever since I got the play into Godolphin's hands. I haven't been at peace about him since that day when he renounced me in Magnolia, and certainly till we got his check there has been nothing in his performance to restore my confidence. Come, now, Louise, you mustn't stop me, dear," he said, for she was beginning to cling about him. "I shall be back for lunch, and then we can talk over what I have begun to do. If I began to talk of it before, I should lose all heart for it. Kiss me good luck!"

She kissed him enough for all the luck in the world, and then he got himself out of her arms while she still hardly knew what to make of it all. He was half-way down the house-stairs, when her eye fell on the prompt-book. She caught it up and ran out upon the landing, and screamed down after him, "Brice, Brice! You've forgotten something."

He came flying back, breathless, and she held the book out to him. "Oh, I don't want that," he panted, "It would damage the play with a manager to know that Godolphin had rejected it."

"But do you think it would be quite right—quite frank—to let him take it without telling him?"

"It will be right to show it him without telling him. It will be time enough to tell him if he likes it."

"That is true," she assented, and then she kissed him again and let him go; he stood a step below her, and she had to stoop a good deal; but she went in doors, looking up to him as if he were a whole flight of steps above her, and saying to herself that he had always been so good and wise that she must now simply trust him in everything.

Louise still had it on her conscience to offer Maxwell reparation for the wrong she thought she had done him when she had once decided that he was too self-seeking and self-centred, and had potentially rejected him on that ground. The first thing she did after they became engaged was to confess the wrong, and give him a chance to cast her off if he wished; but this never seemed quite reparation enough, perhaps because he laughed and said that she was perfectly right about him, and must take him with those faults or not at all. She now entered upon a long, delightful review of his behavior ever since that moment, and she found that, although he was certainly as self-centred as she had ever thought or he had owned himself to be, self-seeking he was not, in any mean or greedy sense. She perceived that his self-seeking, now, at least, was as much for her sake as his own, and that it was really after all not self-seeking, but the helpless pursuit of aims which he was born into the world to achieve. She had seen that he did not stoop to achieve them, but had as haughty a disdain of any but the highest means as she could have wished him to have, and much haughtier than she could have had in his place. If he forgot her in them, he forgot himself quite as much, and they were equal before his ambition. In fact, this seemed to her even more her charge than his, and if he did not succeed as with his genius he had a right to succeed, it would be constructively her fault, and at any rate she should hold herself to blame for it; there would be some satisfaction in that. She thought with tender pathos how hard he worked, and was at his writing all day long, except when she made him go out with her, and was then often so fagged that he could scarcely speak. She was proud of his almost killing himself at it, but she must study more and more not to let him kill himself, and must do everything that was humanly possible to keep up his spirits when he met with a reverse.

She accused herself with shame of having done nothing for

him in the present emergency, but rather flung upon him the burden of her own disappointment. She thought how valiantly he had risen up under it, and had not lost one moment in vain repining; how instantly he had collected himself for a new effort, and taken his measures with a wise prevision that omitted no detail. In view of all this, she peremptorily forbade herself to be uneasy at the little reticence he was practising with regard to Godolphin's having rejected his play; and imagined the splendor he could put on with the manager after he had accepted it, in telling him its history, and releasing him, if he would, from his agreement. She imagined the manager generously saying this made no difference whatever, though he appreciated Mr. Maxwell's candor in the matter, and should be all the happier to make a success of it because Godolphin had failed with it.

But she returned from this flight into the future, and her husband's part in it, to the present and her own first duty in regard to him; and it appeared to her, that this was to look carefully after his health in the strain put upon it, and to nourish him for the struggle before him. It was to be not with one manager only, but many managers, probably, and possibly with all the managers in New York. That was what he had said it would be before he gave up, and she remembered how flushed and excited he looked when he said it, and though she did not believe he would get back for lunch—the manager might ask him to read his play to him, so that he could get just the author's notion—she tried to think out the very most nourishing lunch she could for him. Oysters were in season, and they were very nourishing, but they had already had them for breakfast, and beefsteak was very good, but he hated it. Perhaps chops would do, or, better still, mushrooms on toast, only they were not in the market at that time of year. She dismissed a stewed squab, and questioned a sweetbread, and wondered if there were not some kind of game. In the end she decided to leave it to the provision man, and she lost no time after she reached her decision in going out to consult him. He was a bland, soothing German, and it was a pleasure to talk with him, because he brought her married name into every sentence, and said, "No, Mrs. Maxwell;" "Yes, Mrs. Maxwell;" "I send it right in, Mrs. Maxwell." She went over his whole list of provisions with him, and let him persuade her that a small fillet was the best she could offer a person whose frame needed nourishing, while at the same time his appetite needed coaxing. She allowed him to add a can of mushrooms, as the right thing to go with it, and some salad; and then while he put the order up she stood reproaching herself for it, since it formed no fit lunch, and was both expensive and commonplace.

She was roused from her daze, when she was going to countermand the whole stupid order by the man's saying: "What can I do for you this morning, Mrs. Harley?" and she turned round to find at her elbow the smouldering-eyed woman of the bathing-beach. She lifted her heavy lids and gave Louise a dull glance, which she let a sudden recognition burn through for a moment and then quenched. But in that moment the two women sealed a dislike that had been merely potential before. Their look said for each that the other was by nature, tradition, and aspiration whatever was most detestable in their sex.

Mrs. Harley, whoever she was, under a name that Louise electrically decided to be fictitious, seemed unable to find her voice at first in their mutual defiance, and she made a pretence of letting her strange eyes rove about the shop before she answered. Her presence was so repugnant to Louise that she turned abruptly and hurried out of the place without returning the good-morning which the German sent after her with the usual addition of her name. She resented it now, for if it was not tantamount to an introduction to that creature, it was making her known to her, and Louise wished to have no closer acquaintance with her than their common humanity involved. It seemed too odious to have been again made aware that they were inhabitants of the same planet, and the anger that heaved within her went out in a wild flash of resentment towards her husband for having forever fixed that woman in her consciousness with a phrase. If it had not been for that, she would not have thought twice of her when they first saw her, and she would not have known her when they met again, and at the worst would merely have been harassed with a vague resemblance which would never have been verified.

She had climbed the stairs to their apartment on the fourth floor, when she felt the need to see more, know more, of this hateful being so strong upon her, that she stopped with her latch-key in her door and went down again. She did not formulate her intention, but she meant to hurry back to the provision store, with the pretext of changing her order, and follow the woman wherever she went, until she found out where she lived; and she did not feel, as a man would, the disgrace of dogging her steps in that way so much as she felt a fatal dread of her. If she should be gone by the time Louise got back to the shop, she would ask the provision man about her, and find out in that way. She stayed a little while to rehearse the terms of her inquiry, and while she lingered the woman herself came round the corner of the avenue and mounted the steps where Louise stood and, with an air of custom, went on upstairs to the second floor, where Louise heard her putting a latch-key into the door, which then closed after her.

W. D. Howells

XIII

Maxwell went to a manager whom he had once met in Boston, where they had been apparently acceptable to each other in a long talk they had about the drama. The manager showed himself a shrewd and rather remorseless man of business in all that he said of the theatre, but he spoke as generously and reverently of the drama as Maxwell felt, and they parted with a laughing promise to do something for it yet. In fact, if it had not been for the chances that threw him into Godolphin's hand afterwards, he would have gone to this manager with his play in the first place, and he went to him now, as soon as he was out of Godolphin's hands, not merely because he was the only manager he knew in the city, but because he believed in him as much as his rather sceptical temper permitted him to believe in any one, and because he believed he would give him at least an intelligent audience.

The man in the box-office, where he stood in the glow of an electric light at midday, recovered himself from the disappointment he suffered when Maxwell asked for the manager instead of a seat for the night's performance. He owned that the manager was in his room, but said he was very much engaged, and he was hardly moved from this conviction by Maxwell's urgence that he should send in his card; perhaps something in Maxwell's tone and face as of authority prevailed with him; perhaps it was the title of the Boston

Abstract, which Maxwell wrote under his name, to recall himself better to the manager's memory. The answer was a good while getting back; people came in and bought tickets and went away, while Maxwell hung about the vestibule of the theatre and studied the bill of the play which formed its present attraction, but at last the man in the box-office put his face sidewise to the semi-circular opening above the glass-framed plan of seats and, after he had identified Maxwell, said, "Mr. Grayson would like to see you." At the same time the swinging doors of the theatre opened, and a young man came out, to whom the other added, indicating Maxwell, "This is the gentleman;" and the young man held the door open for him to pass in, and then went swiftly before him into the theatre, and led the way around the orchestra circle to a little door that opened in the wall beside one of the boxes. There was a rehearsal going on in the glare of some grouped incandescent bulbs on the stage, and people moving about in top hats and bonnets and other every-day outside gear, which Maxwell lost sight of in his progress through the wings and past a rough brick wall before he arrived at another door down some winding stairs in the depths of the building. His guide knocked at it, and when an answering voice said, "Come in!" he left Maxwell to go in alone. The manager had risen from his chair at his table, and stood, holding out his hand, with a smile of kindly enough welcome. He said, "I've just made you out, Mr. Maxwell. Do you come as a friendly interviewer, or as a deadly dramatist!"

"As both or as neither, whichever you like," said Maxwell, and he gladly took the manager's hand, and then took the chair which he cleared of some prompt-books for him to sit down in.

"I hadn't forgotten the pleasant talk I had with you in Boston, you see," the manager began again, "but I had forgotten whom I had it with."

"I can't say I had even done that," Maxwell answered, and this seemed to please the manager.

"Well, that counts you one," he said. "You noticed that we have put on 'Engaged?' We've made a failure of the piece we began with; it's several pieces now. *Couldn't* you do something like 'Engaged?'"

"I wish I could! But I'm afraid Gilbert is the only man living who can do anything like 'Engaged.' My hand is too heavy for that kind."

"Well, the heavy hand is not so bad if it hits hard enough," said the manager, who had a face of lively intelligence and an air of wary kindliness. He looked fifty, but this was partly the effect of overwork. There was something of the Jew, something of the Irishman, in his visage; but he was neither; he was a Yankee, from Maine, with a Boston training in his business. "What have you got?" he asked, for Maxwell's play was evident.

"Something I've been at work on for a year, more or less." Maxwell sketched the plot of his play, and the manager seemed interested.

"Rather Ibsenish, isn't it?" he suggested at the end.

The time had passed with Maxwell when he wished to have this said of his play, not because he did not admire Ibsen, but because he preferred the recognition of the original quality of his work. "I don't know that it is, very. Perhaps—if one didn't like it."

"Oh, I don't know that I should dislike it for its Ibsenism.

The time of that sort of thing may be coming. You never can be sure, in this business, when the time of anything is coming. I've always thought that a naturalized Ibsenism wouldn't be so bad for our stage. You don't want to be quite so bleak, you know, as the real Norwegian Ibsen."

"I've tried not to be very bleak, because I thought it wasn't in the scheme," said Maxwell.

"I don't understand that it ends well?"

"Unless you consider the implicated marriage of the young people a good ending. Haxard himself, of course, is past all surgery. But the thing isn't pessimistic, as I understand, for its doctrine is that harm comes only from doing wrong."

The manager laughed. "Oh, the average public would consider that *very* pessimistic. They want no harm to come even from doing wrong. They want the drama to get round it, somehow. If you could show that Divine Providence forgets wrong-doing altogether in certain cases, you would make the fortune of your piece. Come, why couldn't you try something of that kind? It would be the greatest comfort to all the sinners in front, for every last man of them—or woman—would think she was the one who was going to get away."

"I might come up to that, later," said Maxwell, willing to take the humorous view of the matter, if it would please the manager and smooth the way for the consideration of his work; but, more obscurely, he was impatient, and sorry to have found him in so philosophical a mood.

The manager was like the man of any other trade; he liked to talk of his business, and this morning he talked of it a long time, and to an effect that Maxwell must have found useful if he had not been so bent upon getting to his manuscript that

W. D. Howells

he had no mind for generalities. At last the manager said, abruptly, "You want me to read your play?"

"Very much," Maxwell answered, and he promptly put the packet he had brought into the manager's extended hand.

He not only took it, but he untied it, and even glanced at the first few pages. "All right," he said, "I'll read it, and let you hear from me as soon as I can. Your address—oh, it's on the wrapper, here. By-the-way, why shouldn't you lunch with me? We'll go over to the Players' Club."

Maxwell flushed with eager joy; then he faltered.

"I should like to do it immensely. But I'm afraid—I'm afraid Mrs. Maxwell will be waiting for me."

"Oh, all right; some other time," answered the manager; and then Maxwell was vexed that he had offered any excuse, for he thought it would have been very pleasant and perhaps useful for him to lunch at the Players'. But the manager did not urge him. He only said, as he led the way to the stage-door, "I didn't know there was a Mrs. Maxwell."

"She's happened since we met," said Maxwell, blushing with fond pride. "We're such a small family that we like to get together at lunch," he added.

"Oh, yes, I can understand that stage of it," said the manager. "By-the-way, are you still connected with the *Abstract*? I noticed the name on your card."

"Not quite in the old way. But," and with the words a purpose formed itself in Maxwell's mind, "they've asked me to write their New York letter."

"Well, drop in now and then. I may have something for you." The manager shook hands with him cordially, and Maxwell opened the door and found himself in the street.

He was so little conscious of the transit homeward that he seemed to find himself the next moment with Louise in their little parlor. He remembered afterwards that there was something strange in her manner towards him at first, but, before he could feel presently cognizant of it, this wore off in the interest of what he had to tell.

"The sum of it all," he ended his account of the interview with the manager, "is that he's taken the thing to read, and that he's to let me hear from him when he's read it. When that will be nobody knows, and I should be the last to ask. But he seemed interested in my sketch of it, and he had an intelligence about it that was consoling. And it was a great comfort, after Godolphin, and Godolphin's pyrotechnics, to have him take it in a hard, business way. He made no sort of promises, and he held out no sort of hopes; he didn't commit himself in any sort of way, and he can't break his word, for he hasn't given it. I wish, now, that I had never let Godolphin have the play back after he first renounced it; I should have saved a great deal of time and wear and tear of feelings. Yes, if I had taken your advice then—"

At this generous tribute to her wisdom, all that was reluctant ceased from Louise's manner and behavior. She put her arm around his neck and protested. "No, no! I can't let you say that, Brice! You were right about that, as you are about everything. If you hadn't had this experience with Godolphin, you wouldn't have known how to appreciate Mr. Grayson's reception of you, and you might have been unreasonable. I can see now that it's all been for the best, and that we needed just this discipline to prepare us for prosperity. But I guess Godolphin will wish, when he hears that Mr. Grayson has taken your piece, and is going to bring it out at the Argosy, here—"

"Oh, good heavens! Do give those poor chickens a chance to get out of the shell this time, my dear!"

"Well, I know it vexes you, and I know it's silly; but still I feel sure that Mr. Grayson will take it. You don't mind that, do you?"

"Not if you don't say it. I want you to realize that the chances are altogether against it. He was civil, because I think he rather liked me personally—"

"Of *course* he did!"

"Oh!"

"Well, never mind. Personally—"

"And I don't suppose it did me any harm with him to suppose that I still had a newspaper connection. I put Boston *Abstract* on my card—for purposes of identification, as the editors say—because I was writing for it when I met him in Boston."

"Oh, well, as long as you're not writing for it now, I don't care. I want you to devote yourself entirely to the drama, Brice."

"Yes, that's all very well. But I think I shall do Ricker's letters for him this winter at least. I was thinking of it on the way down. It'll be work, but it'll be money, too, and if I have something coming in I sha'n't feel as if I were ruined every time my play gets back from a manager."

"Mr. Grayson will take it!"

"Now, Louise, if you say that, you will simply drive me to despair, for I shall know how you will feel when he doesn't—"

"No, I shall not feel so; and you will see. But if you don't let me hope for you—"

"You know I can't stand hoping. The only safe way is to look for the worst, and if anything better happens it is so much pure gain. If we hadn't been so eager to pin our faith to Godolphin—"

"How much better off should we have been? What have we lost by it?" she challenged him.

He broke off with a laugh. "We have lost the pins. Well, hope away! But, remember, you take the whole responsibility." Maxwell pulled out his watch. "Isn't lunch nearly ready? This prosperity is making me hungry, and it seems about a year since breakfast."

"I'll see what's keeping it," said Louise, and she ran out to the kitchen with a sudden fear in her heart. She knew that she had meant to countermand her order for the fillet and mushrooms, and she thought that she had forgotten to order anything else for lunch. She found the cook just serving it up, because such a dish as that took more time than an ordinary lunch, and the things had come late. Louise said, Yes, she understood that; and went back to Maxwell, whom she found walking up and down the room in a famine very uncommon for him. She felt the motherly joy a woman has in being able to appease the hunger of the man she loves, and now she was glad that she had not postponed the fillet till dinner as she had thought of doing. Everything was turning out so entirely for the best that she was beginning to experience some revival of an ancestral faith in Providence in a heart individually agnostic, and she was piously happy when Maxwell said at sight of the lunch, "Isn't this rather prophetic? If it isn't that, it's telepathic. I sha'n't regret now that I didn't go with Grayson to lunch at the Players' Club."

"Did he ask you to do that?"

Maxwell nodded with his mouth full.

A sudden misgiving smote her. "Oh, Brice, you ought to have gone! Why didn't you go?"

"It must have been a deep subconsciousness of the fillet and mushrooms. Or perhaps I didn't quite like to think of your lunching alone."

"Oh, you dear, faithful little soul!" she cried. The tears came into her eyes, and she ran round the table to kiss him several times on the top of his head.

He kept on eating as well as he could, and when she got back to her place, "Of course, it would have been a good thing for me to go to the Players'," he teased, "for it would have pleased Grayson, and I should probably have met some other actors and managers there, and made interest with them provisionally for my play, if he shouldn't happen to want it."

"Oh, I know it," she moaned. "You have ruined yourself for me. I'm not worth it. No, I'm not! Now, I want you to promise, dearest, that you'll never mind me again, but lunch or dine, or breakfast, or sup whenever anybody asks you?"

"Well, I can't promise all that, quite."

"I mean, when the play is at stake."

"Oh, in that case, yes."

"What in the world did you say to Mr. Grayson?"

"Very much what I have said to you: that I hated to leave you to lunch alone here."

"Oh, didn't he think it very silly?" she entreated, fondly. "Don't you think he'll laugh at you for it!"

"Very likely. But he won't like me the less for it. Men are glad of marital devotion in other men; they feel that it acts as a sort of dispensation for them."

"You oughtn't to waste those things on me," she said, humbly. "You ought to keep them for your plays."

"Oh, they're not wasted, exactly. I can use them over again. I can say much better things than that with a pen in my hand."

She hardly heard him. She felt a keen remorse for something she had meant to do and to say when he came home. Now she put it far from her; she thought she ought not to keep even an extinct suspicion in her heart against him, and she asked, "Brice, did you know that woman was living in this house?"

"What woman?"

Louise was ashamed to say anything about the smouldering eyes. "That woman on the bathing-beach at Magnolia—the one I met the other day."

He said, dryly: "She seems to be pursuing us. How did you find it out?"

She told him, and she added, "I think she *must* be an actress of some sort."

"Very likely, but I hope she won't feel obliged to call because we're connected with the profession."

Some time afterwards Louise was stitching at a centre-piece she was embroidering for the dining-table, and Maxwell was writing a letter for the *Abstract*, which he was going to send to the editor with a note telling him that if it were the sort of thing he wanted he would do the letters for them.

"After all," she breathed, "that look of the eyes may be purely physical."

"What look?" Maxwell asked, from the depths of his work.

She laughed in perfect content, and said: "Oh, nothing." But when he finished his letter, and was putting it into the envelope, she asked: "Did you tell Mr. Grayson that Godolphin had returned the play?"

"No, I didn't. That wasn't necessary at this stage of the proceedings."

"No."

XIV

During the week that passed before Maxwell heard from the manager concerning his play, he did another letter for the *Abstract*, and, with a journalistic acquaintance enlarged through certain Boston men who had found places on New York papers, familiarized himself with New York ways and means of getting news. He visited what is called the Coast, a series of points where the latest intelligence grows in hotel bars and lobbies of a favorable exposure, and is nurtured by clerks and barkeepers skilled in its culture, and by inveterate gossips of their acquaintance; but he found this sort of stuff generally telegraphed on by the Associated Press before he reached it, and he preferred to make his letter a lively comment on events, rather than a report of them. The editor of the *Abstract* seemed to prefer this, too. He wrote Maxwell some excellent criticism, and invited him to appeal to the better rather than the worse curiosity of his readers, to remember that this was the principle of the *Abstract* in its home conduct. Maxwell showed the letter to his wife, and she approved of it all so heartily that she would have liked to answer it herself. "Of course, Brice," she said, "it's *you* he wants, more than your news. Any wretched reporter could give him that, but you are the one man in the world who can give him your mind about it."

"Why not say universe?" returned Maxwell, but though he

mocked her he was glad to believe she was right, and he was proud of her faith in him.

In another way this was put to proof more than once during the week, for Louise seemed fated to meet Mrs. Harley on the common stairs now when she went out or came in. It was very strange that after living with her a whole month in the house and not seeing her, she should now be seeing her so much. Mostly she was alone, but sometimes she was with an elderly woman, whom Louise decided at one time to be her mother, and at another time to be a professional companion. The first time she met them together she was sure that Mrs. Harley indicated her to the chaperon, and that she remembered her from Magnolia, but she never looked at Louise, any more than Louise looked at her, after that.

She wondered if Maxwell ever met her, but she was ashamed to ask him, and he did not mention her. Only once when they were together did they happen to encounter her, and then he said, quite simply, "I think she's certainly an actress. That public look of the eyes is unmistakable. Emotional parts, I should say."

Louise forced herself to suggest, "You might get her to let you do a play for her."

"I doubt if I could do anything unwholesome enough for her."

At last the summons they were expecting from Grayson came, just after they had made up their minds to wait another week for it.

Louise had taken the letter from the maid, and she handed it to Maxwell with a gasp at sight of the Argosy theatre address printed in the corner of the envelope. "I know it's a refusal."

"If you think that will make it an acceptance," he had the hardihood to answer, "it won't. I've tried that sort of thing too often;" and he tore open the letter.

It was neither a refusal nor an acceptance, and their hopes soared again, hers visibly, his secretly, to find it a friendly confession that the manager had not found time to read the play until the night before, and a request that Maxwell would drop in any day between twelve and one, which was rather a leisure time with him, and talk it over.

"Don't lose an instant, dear!" she adjured him.

"It's only nine o'clock," he answered, "and I shall have to lose several instants."

"That is so," she lamented; and then they began to canvas the probable intention of the manager's note. She held out passionately to the end for the most encouraging inter-pretation of it, but she did not feel that it would have any malign effect upon the fact for him to say, "Oh, it's just a way of letting me down easy," and it clearly gave him great heart to say so.

When he went off to meet his fate, she watched him, trembling, from the window; as she saw him mounting the elevated steps, she wondered at his courage; she had given him all her own.

The manager met him with "Ah, I'm glad you came soon. These things fade out of one's mind so, and I really want to talk about your play. I've been very much interested in it."

Maxwell could only bow his head and murmur something about being very glad, very, very glad, with a stupid iteration.

W. D. Howells

"I suppose you know, as well as I do, that it's two plays, and that it's only half as good as if it were one."

The manager wheeled around from his table, and looked keenly at the author, who contrived to say, "I think I know what you mean."

"You've got the making of the prettiest kind of little comedy in it, and you've got the making of a very strong tragedy. But I don't think your oil and water mix, exactly," said Grayson.

"You think the interest of the love-business will detract from the interest of the homicide's fate?"

"And vice versa. Excuse me for asking something that I can very well understand your not wanting to tell till I had read your play. Isn't this the piece Godolphin has been trying out West?"

"Yes, it is," said Maxwell. "I thought it might prejudice you against it, if—"

"Oh, that's all right. Why have you taken it from him?"

Maxwell felt that he could make up for his want of earlier frankness now. "I didn't take it from him; he gave it back to me."

He sketched the history of his relation to the actor, and the manager said, with smiling relish, "Just like him, just like Godolphin." Then he added, "I'll tell you, and you mustn't take it amiss. Godolphin may not know just why he gave the piece up, and he probably thinks it's something altogether different, but you may depend upon it the trouble was your trying to ride two horses in it. Didn't you feel that it was a mistake yourself?"

"I felt it so strongly at one time that I decided to develop the love-business into a play by itself and let the other go for some other time. My wife and I talked it over. We even discussed it with Godolphin. He wanted to do Atland. But we all backed out simultaneously, and went back to the play as it stood."

"Godolphin saw he couldn't make enough of Atland," said the manager, as if he were saying it to himself. "Well, you may be sure he feels now that the character which most appeals to the public in the play is Salome."

"He felt that before."

"And he was right. Now, I will tell you what you have got to do. You have either got to separate the love-business from the rest of the play and develop it into a comedy by itself—"

"That would mean a great deal of work, and I am rather sick of the whole thing."

"Or," the manager went on without minding Maxwell, "you have got to cut the part of Salome, and subordinate it entirely to Haxard"—Maxwell made a movement of impatience and refusal, and the manager finished—"or else you have got to treat it frankly as the leading part in the piece, and get it into the hands of some leading actress."

"Do you mean," the author asked, "that you—or any manager—would take it if that were done?"

Grayson looked a little unhappy. "No, that isn't what I mean, exactly. I mean that as it stands, no manager would risk it, and that as soon as an actor had read it, he would see, as Godolphin must have seen from the start, that Haxard was a subordinate part. What you want to do is to get it in the hands of some woman who wants to star, and would take the road with it." The manager expatiated at some length on the point, and then he stopped, and sat silent, as if he had done with the subject.

Maxwell perceived that the time had come for him to get up and go away.

"I'm greatly obliged to you for all your kindness, Mr. Grayson, and I won't abuse your patience any further. You've been awfully good to me, and—" He faltered, in a dejection which he could not control. Against all reason, he had hoped that the manager would have taken his piece just as it stood, and apparently he would not have taken it in any event.

"You mustn't speak of that," said the manager. "I wish you would let me see anything else you do. There's a great deal that's good in this piece, and I believe that a woman who would make it her battle-horse could make it go."

Maxwell asked, with melancholy scorn, "But you don't happen to know any leading lady who is looking round for a battle-horse?"

The manager seemed trying to think. "Yes, I do. You wouldn't like her altogether, and I don't say she would be the ideal Salome, but she would be, in her way, effective; and I know that she wants very much to get a play. She hasn't been doing anything for a year or two but getting married and divorced, but she made a very good start. She used to call herself Yolande Havisham; I don't suppose it was her name; and she had a good deal of success in the West; I don't think she's ever appeared in New York. I believe she was of quite a good Southern family; the Southerners all are; and I hear she has money."

"Godolphin mentioned a Southern girl for the part," said Maxwell. "I wonder if—"

"Very likely it's the same one. She does emotional leads. She and Godolphin played together in California, I believe. I was trying to think of her married name—or her unmarried name—"

Some one knocked at the door, and the young man put his head in, with what Maxwell fancied a preconcerted effect, and gave the manager a card. He said, "All right; bring him round," and he added to Maxwell, "Shall I send your play—"

"No, no, I will take it," and Maxwell carried it away with a heavier heart than he had even when he got it back from Godolphin. He did not know how to begin again, and he had to go home and take counsel with his wife as to the next step.

He could not bear to tell her of his disappointment, and it was harder still to tell her of the kind of hope the manager had held out to him. He revolved a compromise in his mind, and when they sat down together he did not mean to conceal anything, but only to postpone something; he did not clearly know why. He told her the alternatives the manager had suggested, and she agreed with him they were all impossible.

"Besides," she said, "he doesn't promise to take the play, even if you do everything to a 't.' Did he ask you to lunch again?"

"No, that seemed altogether a thing of the past."

"Well, let us have ours, and then we can go into the Park, and forget all about it for a while, and perhaps something new will suggest itself."

That was what they did, but nothing new suggested itself. They came home fretted with their futile talk. There seemed nothing for Maxwell to do but to begin the next day with some other manager.

They found a note from Grayson waiting Maxwell. "Well, you open it," he said, listlessly, to his wife, and in fact he felt himself at that moment physically unable to cope with the task, and he dreaded any fluctuation of emotion that would follow, even if it were a joyous one.

"What does this mean, Brice?" demanded his wife, with a terrible provisionality in her tone, as she stretched out the letter to him, and stood before him where he lounged in the cushioned window-seat.

Grayson had written: "If you care to submit your play to Yolande Havisham, you can easily do so. I find that her address is the same as yours. Her name is Harley. But I was mistaken about the divorce. It was a death."

Maxwell lay stupidly holding the note before him.

"Will you tell me what it means?" his wife repeated. "Or why you didn't tell me before, if you meant to give your play to that creature?"

"I don't mean to give it to her," said Maxwell, doggedly. "I never did, for an instant. As for not telling you that Grayson had suggested it—well, perhaps I wished to spare myself a scene like the present."

"Do you think I will believe you?"

"I don't think you will insult me. Why shouldn't you believe I am telling you the truth?"

"Because—because you didn't tell me at once."

"That is nonsense, and you know it. If I wanted to keep this from you, it was to spare you the annoyance I can't help now, and because the thing was settled in my mind as soon as Grayson proposed it."

"Then, why has he written to you about it?"

"I suppose I didn't say it was settled."

"Suppose? Don't you *know* whether you did?"

"Come, now, Louise! I am not on the witness-stand, and I won't be cross-questioned. You ought to be ashamed of yourself. What is the matter with you? Am I to blame because a man who doesn't imagine your dislike of a woman that you never spoke to suggests her taking part in a play that she probably wouldn't look at? You're preposterous! Try to have a little common-sense!" These appeals seemed to have a certain effect with his wife; she looked daunted; but Maxwell had the misfortune to add, "One would think you were jealous of the woman."

"*Now* you are insulting *me*!" she cried. "But it's a part of the vulgarity of the whole business. Actors, authors, managers, you're all alike."

Maxwell got very pale. "Look out, Louise!" he warned her.

"I *won't* look out. If you had any delicacy, the least delicacy in the world, you could imagine how a woman who had given the most sacred feelings of her nature to you for your selfish art would loathe to be represented by such a creature as that, and still not be jealous of her, as you call it! But I am justly punished! I might have expected it."

W. D. Howells

The maid appeared at the door and said something, which neither of them could make out at once, but which proved to be the question whether Mrs. Maxwell had ordered the dinner.

"No, I will go—I was just going out for it," said Louise. She had in fact not taken off her hat or gloves since she came in from her walk, and she now turned and swept out of the room without looking at her husband. He longed to detain her, to speak some kindly or clarifying word, to set himself right with her, to set her right with herself; but the rage was so hot in his heart that he could not. She came back to the door a moment, and looked in. "*I* will do *my* duty."

"It's rather late," he sneered, "but if you're very conscientious, I dare say we shall have dinner at the usual time."

He did not leave the window-seat, and it was as if the door had only just clashed to after her when there came a repeated and violent ringing at the bell, so that he jumped up himself, to answer it, without waiting for the maid.

"Your wife—your wife!" panted the bell-boy, who stood there. "She's hurt herself, and she's fainted."

"My wife? Where—how?" He ran down stairs after the boy, and in the hallway on the ground floor he found Louise stretched upon the marble pavement, with her head in the lap of a woman, who was chafing her hands. He needed no look at this woman's face to be sure that it was the woman of his wife's abhorrence, and he felt quite as sure that it was the actress Yolande Havisham, from the effective drama of her self-possession.

"Don't be frightened. Your wife turned her foot on the steps here. I was coming into the house, and caught her from falling. It's only a swoon." She spoke with the pseudo-English accent of the stage, but with a Southern slip upon the vowels here and there. "Get some water, please."

The hall-boy came running up the back stairs with some that he had gone to get, and the woman bade Maxwell sprinkle his wife's face. But he said: "No—you," and he stooped and took his wife's head into his own hands, so that she might not come to in the lap of Mrs. Harley; in the midst of his dismay he reflected how much she would hate that. He could hardly keep himself from being repellant and resentful towards the woman. In his remorse for quarrelling with Louise, it was the least reparation he could offer her. Mrs. Harley, if it were she, seemed not to notice his rudeness. She sprinkled Louise's face, and wiped her forehead with the handkerchief she dipped in the water; but this did not bring her out of her faint, and Maxwell began to think she was dead, and to feel that he was a murderer. With a strange aesthetic vigilance he took note of his sensations for use in revising Haxard.

The janitor of the building had somehow arrived, and Mrs. Harley said: "I will go for a doctor, if you can get her up to your apartment;" and she left Louise with the two men.

The janitor, a burly Irishman, lifted her in his arms, and carried her up the three flights of steps; Maxwell followed, haggardly, helplessly.

On her own bed, Louise revived, and said: "My shoe—Oh, get it off!"

The doctor came a few minutes later, but Mrs. Harley did not appear with him as Maxwell had dreaded she would. He decided that Mrs. Maxwell had strained, not sprained, her ankle, and he explained how the difference was all the difference in the world, as he bound the ankle up with a long

W. D. Howells

ribbon of india-rubber, and issued directions for care and quiet.

He left them there, and Maxwell heard him below in parley, apparently with the actress at her door. Louise lay with her head on her husband's arm, and held his other hand tight in hers, while he knelt by the bed. The bliss of repentance and mutual forgiveness filled both their hearts, while she told him how she had hurt herself.

"I had got down to the last step, and I was putting my foot to the pavement, and I thought, Now I am going to turn my ankle. Wasn't it strange? And I turned it. How did you get me upstairs?"

"The janitor carried you."

"How lucky he happened to be there! I suppose the hall-boy kept me from falling—poor little fellow! You must give him some money. How did you find out about me?"

"He ran up to tell," Maxwell said this, and then he hesitated. "I guess you had better know all about it. Can you bear something disagreeable, or would you rather wait—"

"No, no, tell me now! I can't bear to wait. What is it?"

"It wasn't the hall-boy that caught you. It was that—woman."

He felt her neck and hand grow rigid, but he went on, and told her all about it. At the end some quiet tears came into her eyes. "Well, then, we must be civil to her. I am glad you told me at once, Brice!" She pulled his head down and kissed him, and he was glad, too.

XV

Louise sent Maxwell down to Mrs. Harley's apartment to thank her, and tell her how slight the accident was; and while he was gone she abandoned herself to an impassioned dramatization of her own death from blood-poisoning, and her husband's early marriage with the actress, who then appeared in all his plays, though they were not happy together. Her own spectre was always rising between them, and she got some fearful joy out of that. She counted his absence by her heart-beats, but he came back so soon that she was ashamed, and was afraid that he had behaved so as to give the woman a notion that he was not suffered to stay longer. He explained that he had found her gloved and bonneted to go out, and that he had not stayed for fear of keeping her. She had introduced him to her mother, who was civil about Louise's accident, and they had both begged him to let them do anything they could for her. He made his observations, and when Louise, after a moment, asked him about them, he said they affected him as severally typifying the Old South and the New South. They had a photograph over the mantel, thrown up large, of an officer in Confederate uniform. Otherwise the room had nothing personal in it; he suspected the apartment of having been taken furnished, like their own. Louise asked if he should say they were ladies, and he answered that he thought they were.

W. D. Howells

"Of course," she said, and she added, with a wide sweep of censure: "They get engaged to four or five men at a time, down there. Well," she sighed, "you mustn't stay in here with me, dear. Go to your writing."

"I was thinking whether you couldn't come out and lie on the lounge. I hate to leave you alone in here."

"No, the doctor said to be perfectly quiet. Perhaps I can, to-morrow, if it doesn't swell up any worse."

She kept her hold of his hand, which he had laid in hers, and he sat down beside the bed, in the chair he had left there. He did not speak, and after a while she asked, "What are you thinking of?"

"Oh, nothing. The confounded play, I suppose."

"You're disappointed at Grayson's not taking it."

"One is always a fool."

"Yes," said Louise, with a catching of the breath. She gripped his hand hard, and said, as well as she could in keeping back the tears, "Well, I will never stand in your way, Brice. You may do anything—*anything*—with it that you think best."

"I shall never do anything you don't like," he answered, and he leaned over and kissed her, and at this her passion burst in a violent sobbing, and when she could speak she made him solemnly promise that he would not regard her in the least, but would do whatever was wisest and best with the play, for otherwise she should never be happy again.

As she could not come out to join him at dinner, he brought a little table to the bedside, and put his plate on it, and ate his dinner there with her. She gave him some attractive morsels off her own plate, which he had first insisted on bestowing upon her. They had such a gay evening that the future brightened again, and they arranged for Maxwell to take his play down-town the next day, and not lose a moment in trying to place it with some manager.

It all left him very wakeful, for his head began to work upon this scheme and that. When he went to lock the outer door for the night, the sight of his overcoat hanging in the hall made him think of a theatrical newspaper he had bought coming home, at a certain corner of Broadway, where numbers of smooth-shaven, handsome men, and women with dark eyes and champagned hair were lounging and passing. He had got it on the desperate chance that it might suggest something useful to him. He now took it out of his coat-pocket, and began to look its advertisements over in the light of his study lamp, partly because he was curious about it, and partly because he knew that he should begin to revise his play otherwise, and then he should not sleep all night.

In several pages of the paper ladies with flowery and alliterative names and pseudonyms proclaimed themselves in large letters, and in smaller type the parts they were presently playing in different combinations; others gave addresses and announced that they were At Liberty, or specified the kinds of roles they were accustomed to fill, as Leads or Heavies, Dancing Soubrettes and Boys; Leads, Emotional and Juvenile; Heavy or Juvenile or Emotional Leads. There were gentlemen seeking engagements who were Artistic Whistling Soloists, Magicians, Leading Men, Leading Heavies, Singing and Dancing Comedians, and there were both ladies and gentlemen who were now Starring in this play or that, but were open to offers later. A teacher of stage dancing promised instruction in skirt and serpentine dancing, as well as high kicking, front and back, the backward bend, side practice, toe-practice, and all novelties. Dramatic authors had their cards among the rest, and one poor fellow, as if he had not the heart to name himself, advertised a play to be heard of at the office of the newspaper. Whatever related to the theatre was there, in bizarre solidarity, which was droll enough to Maxwell in one way. But he hated to be mixed up with all that, and he perceived that he must be mixed up with it more and more, if he wrote for the theatre. Whether he liked it or not, he was part of the thing which in its entirety meant high-kicking and toe-practice, as well as the expression of the most mystical passions of the heart. There was an austerity in him which the fact offended, and he did what he could to appease this austerity by reflecting that it was the drama and never the theatre that he loved; but for the time this was useless. He saw that if he wrote dramas he could not hold aloof from the theatre, nor from actors and actresses—heavies and juveniles, and emotionals and soubrettes. He must know them, and more intimately; and at first he must be subject to them, however he mastered them at last; he must flatter their oddities and indulge their caprices. His experience with Godolphin had taught him that, and his experience with Godolphin in the construction of his play could be nothing to what he must undergo at rehearsals and in the effort to adapt his work to a company. He reminded himself that Shakespeare even must have undergone all that. But this did not console him. He was himself, and what another, the greatest, had suffered would not save him. Besides, it was not the drama merely that Maxwell loved; it was not making plays alone; it was causing the life that he had known to speak from the stage, and to teach there its serious and important lesson. In the last analysis he was a moralist, and more a moralist than he imagined. To enforce, in the vividest and most palpable form, what he had thought true, it might be worth while to endure all the trials that he must; but at that moment he did not think so; and he did not dare submit his misgiving to his wife.

They had now been six months married, and if he had allowed himself to face the fact he must have owned that, though they loved each other so truly, and he had known moments of exquisite, of incredible rapture, he had been as little happy as in any half-year he had lived. He never formulated his wife's character, or defined the precise relation she bore to his life; if he could have been challenged to do so, he would have said that she was the whole of life to him, and that she was the most delightful woman in the world.

He tasted to its last sweetness the love of loving her and of being loved by her. At the same time there was an obscure stress upon him which he did not trace to her at once; a trouble in his thoughts which, if he could have seen it clearly, he would have recognized for a lurking anxiety concerning how she would take the events of their life as they came. Without realizing it, for his mind was mostly on his work, and it was only in some dim recess of his spirit that the struggle took place, he was perpetually striving to adjust himself to the unexpected, or rather the unpredictable.

But when he was most afraid of her harassing uncertainty of emotion or action he was aware of her fixed loyalty to him; and perhaps it was the final effect with himself that he dreaded. Should he always be able to bear and forbear, as he felt she would, with all her variableness and turning? The question did not put itself in words, and neither did his conviction that his relation to the theatre was doubled in difficulty through her. But he perceived that she had no love for the drama, and only a love for his love of it; and sometimes he vaguely suspected that if he had been in business she would have been as fond of business as she was of the drama. He never perhaps comprehended her ideal, and

W. D. Howells

how it could include an explicit and somewhat noisy devotion to the aims of his ambition, because it was his, and a patronizing reservation in regard to the ambition itself. But this was quite possible with Louise, just as it was possible for her to have had a humble personal joy in giving herself to him, while she had a distinct social sense of the sacrifice she had made in marrying him. In herself she looked up to him; as her father's and mother's daughter, as the child of her circumstance, there is no doubt she looked down upon him. But neither of these attitudes held in their common life. Love may or may not level ranks, but marriage unquestionably does, and is the one form of absolute equality. The Maxwells did not take themselves or each other objectively; they loved and hated, they made war and made peace, without any sense of the difference or desert that might have been apparent to the spectators.

Maxwell had never been so near the standpoint of the impartial observer as now when he confronted the question of what he should do, with a heart twice burdened by the question whether his wife would not make it hard for him to do it, whatever it was. He thought, with dark foreboding, of the difficulties he should have to smooth out for her if it ever came to a production of the piece. The best thing that could happen, perhaps, would be its rejection, final and total, by all possible managers and actors; for she would detest any one who took the part of Salome, and would hold him responsible for all she should suffer from it.

He recurred to what he had felt so strongly himself, and what Grayson had suggested, and thought how he could free himself from fealty to her by cutting out the whole love-business from his play. But that would be very hard. The thing had now knitted itself in one texture in his mind, and though he could sever the ties that bound the parts together, it would take from the piece the great element of charm. It was not symmetrical as it stood, but it was not two distinct motives; the motives had blended, and they really belonged to each other. He would have to invent some other love-business if he cut this out, but still it could be done. Then it suddenly flashed upon him that there was something easier yet, and that was to abandon the notion of getting his piece played at all, and to turn it into a novel. He could give it narrative form without much trouble, if any, beyond that of copying it, and it would be thought a very dramatic story. He saw instantly how he could keep and even enhance all the charm of the love-business as it stood, in a novel; and in his revulsion of feeling he wished to tell his wife. He made a movement towards the door of her room, but he heard the even breathing of her sleep, and he stopped and flung himself on the lounge to think. It was such a happy solution of the whole affair! He need not even cease trying it with the managers, for he could use the copy of the play that Godolphin had returned for that, and he could use the copy he had always kept for recasting it in narrative. By the time that he had got his play back from the last manager he would have his novel ready for the first publisher. In the meantime he should be writing his letters for the *Abstract*, and not consuming all his little savings.

The relief from the stress upon him was delicious. He lay at rest and heard the soft breathing of his wife from the other room, and an indescribable tenderness for her filled his heart. Then he heard her voice saying, "Well, don't wake him, poor boy!"

W. D. Howells

XVI

Maxwell opened his eyes and found the maid lightly escaping from the room. He perceived that he had slept all night on the lounge, and he sent a cheery hail into his wife's room, and then followed it to tell her how he had thought it all out. She was as glad as he was; she applauded his plan to the ceiling; and he might not have thought of her accident if he had not seen presently that she was eating her breakfast in bed.

Then he asked after her ankle, and she said, "Oh, that is perfectly well, or the same as perfectly. There's no pain at all there to speak of, and I shall get up to luncheon. You needn't mind me any more. If you haven't taken your death of cold sleeping there on the lounge—"

"I haven't."

"I want you to go down town to some manager with your play, and get some paper, the kind I like; and then, after lunch, we'll begin turning it into a novel, from your copy. It will be so easy for you that you can dictate, and I'll do the writing, and we'll work it up together. Shall you like collaborating with me?"

"Ah!—"

"It will be our story, and I shall like it twice as well as if it were a play. We shall be independent of the theatre, that's one satisfaction; they can take the play, if they like, but it will be perfectly indifferent to us. I shall help you get in all those nice touches that you said you could never get into a play, like that green light in the woods. I know just how we shall manage that love business, and we sha'n't have any horror of an actress interpreting our inspirations to the public. We'll play Atland and Salome ourselves. We'll— ow!"

She had given her foot a twist in the excitement and she fell back on the pillow rather faint. But she instantly recovered herself with a laugh, and she hurried him away to his breakfast, and then away with his play. He would rather have stayed and begun turning it into a story at once. But she would not let him; she said it would be a loss of time, and she should fret a good deal more to have him there with her, than to have him away, for she should know he was just staying to cheer her up.

When he was gone she sent for whatever papers the maid could find in the parlor, so that she need not think of him in the amusement she would get out of them. Among the rest was that dramatic newspaper which caught her eye first, with the effigy of a very dramatized young woman whose portrait filled the whole first page. Louise abhorred her, but with a novel sense of security in the fact that Maxwell's play was going so soon to be turned into a story; and she felt personally aloof from all the people who had dragged him down with a sense of complicity in their professional cards. She found them neither so droll nor so painful as he had, but she was very willing to turn from them, and she was giving the paper a parting glance before dropping it when she was arrested by an advertisement which made her start:

WANTED.—A drama for prominent star; light comic and emotional: star part must embody situations for the display of intense effects. Address L. STERNE, this office.

A series of effects as intense as the advertiser could have desired in a drama followed one another in the mind of Louise. She now wildly reproached herself that she had, however unwittingly, sent her husband out of reach for four or five hours, when his whole future might depend upon his instantly answering this notice. Whether he had already seen the notice and rashly decided to ignore it, or had not seen it, he might involve himself with some manager irretrievably before he could be got at with a demand which seemed specifically framed to describe his play. She was in despair that there was no means of sending a messenger-boy after him with any chance of finding him. The light comic reliefs which the advertiser would have wished to give the dark phases of her mood were suggested by her reckless energy in whirling herself into her dressing-gown, and hopping out to Maxwell's desk in the other room, where she dashed off a note in reply to the advertisement in her husband's name, and then checked herself with the reflection that she had no right to sign his name: even in such a cause she must not do anything wrong. Something must be done, however, right or wrong, and she decided that a very formal note in the third person would involve the least moral trespass. She fixed upon these terms, after several experiments, almost weeping at the time they cost her, when every moment was precious:

Mr. Brice Maxwell writes to Mr. L. Sterne and begs to inform him that he has a play which he believes will meet the requirements of Mr. Sterne, as stated in his advertisement in the Theatrical Register of November the tenth. Mr. Maxwell asks the favor of an interview with Mr. Sterne at any time and place that Mr. Sterne may appoint.

It seemed to her that this violated no law of man or God, or if it did the exigency was such that the action could be forgiven, if not justified. She ransacked Maxwell's desk for a special delivery stamp, and sent the letter out beyond recall; and then it occurred to her that its opening terms were too much those of a lady addressing a seamstress; but after a good deal of anguish on this point she comforted herself with the hope that a man would not know the form, or at least would not suspect another man of using it offensively.

She passed the time till Maxwell came back, in doubt whether to tell him what she had done. There was no reason why she should not, except that he might have seen the advertisement and decided not to answer it for some reason; but in that case it might be said that he ought to have spoken to her about it. She told him everything at once, but there were many things that he did not tell her till long afterwards; it would be a good thing to let him realize how that felt; besides, it would be a pleasure to keep it and let it burst upon him, if that L. Sterne, whoever he was, asked to see the play. In any case, it would not be a great while that she need keep from him what she had done, but at sight of him when he came in she could hardly be silent. He was gloomy and dispirited, and he confessed that his pleasant experience with Grayson had not been repeated with the other managers. They had all been civil enough, and he had seen three or four of them, but only one had consented to let him even leave his play with him; the others said that it would be useless for them to look at it.

She could not forbear showing him the advertisement she had answered as they sat at lunch; but he glanced at it with disdain, and said there must be some sort of fake in it; if it was some irresponsible fellow getting up a combination he would not scruple to use the ideas of any manuscript submitted to him and work them over to suit himself. Louise could not speak. All heart went out of her; she wanted to cry, and she did not tell what she had done.

Neither of them ate much. He asked her if she was ready to begin on the story with him; she said, "Oh yes;" and she hobbled off into the other room. Then he seemed to remember her hurt for the first time; he had been so full of his failure with the play before. He asked her how she was, and she said much better; and then he stretched himself on the lounge and tried to dictate, and she took her place at his desk and tried to write. But she either ran ahead of him and prompted him, which vexed him, or she lagged so far behind that he lost the thread of what he was saying and became angry. At last she put her head down on the paper and blotted it with her tears.

At that he said, "Oh, you'd better go back to bed," and then, though he spoke harshly, he lifted her tenderly and half carried her to her room.

XVII

They did not try working the play into a story again together. Maxwell kept doggedly at it, though he said it was of no use; the thing had taken the dramatic form with inexorable fixity as it first came from his mind; it could be changed, of course, but it could only be changed for the worse, artistically. If he could sell it as a story, the work would not be lost; he would gain the skill that came from doing, in any event, and it would keep him alive under the ill-luck that now seemed to have set in.

None of the managers wanted his play. Some of them seemed to want it less than others; some wanted it less immediately than others; some did not want it after reading; some refused it without reading it; some had their arrangements made for an indefinite time, others in the present uncertain state of affairs could not make any arrangements; some said it was an American play; others that it was un-American in its pessimistic spirit; some found it too literary; others, lacking in imagination. They were nearly all so kind that at first Maxwell was guilty of the folly of trying to persuade them against the reasons they gave; when he realized that these reasons were also excuses, he set his teeth and accepted them in silence.

For a number of days Louise suffered in momentary

W. D. Howells

expectation of a reply from L. Sterne. She thought it would come by district messenger the day she wrote; and for several days afterwards she had the letters brought to her first, so that she could read them, and not disturb Maxwell with them at his work, if it were not necessary. He willingly agreed to that; he saw that it helped to pass the irksome time for her. She did not mean to conceal any answer she should have from L. Sterne, but she meant when the answer came to prepare her husband for it in such sort that he would understand her motive, and though he condemned it, would easily forgive her. But the days went and no letter from L. Sterne came, and after a season of lively indignation at his rudeness, Louise began to forget him a little, though she still kept her surveillance of the mail.

It was always on her conscience, in the meantime, to give some of the first moments of her recovery to going with Maxwell and thanking Mrs. Harley for the kindness she had shown her in her accident. She was the more strenuous in this intention because the duty was so distasteful, and she insisted upon Maxwell's company, though he argued that he had already done enough himself in thanking her preserver, because she wished to punish a certain reluctance of her own in having him go. She promised herself that she would do everything that was right by the creature; and perhaps she repaired to her presence in rather overwhelming virtue. If this was so, Mrs. Harley showed herself equal to the demand upon her, and was overwhelming in her kind. She not only made nothing of what she had done for Louise, but she made nothing of Louise, and contrived with a few well-directed strokes to give her distinctly the sense of being a chit, a thing Louise was not at all used to. She was apparently one of those women who have no use for persons of their own sex; but few women, even of that sort, could have so promptly relegated Louise to the outside of their interest, or so frankly devoted themselves to Maxwell. The impartial spectator might easily have imagined that it was his ankle which had been strained, and that Louise was at best an intrusive sympathizer. Sometimes Mrs. Harley did not hear what she said; at other times, if she began a response to her, she ended it in a question to him; even when she talked to Louise, her eyes were smouldering upon Maxwell. If this had all or any of it been helpless or ignorant rudeness, it could have been borne and forgiven; but Louise was aware of intention, of perfect intelligence in it; she was sensible of being even more disliked than disliking, and of finally being put to flight with a patronizing benevolence for her complete recovery that was intolerable. What was worse was that, while the woman had been so offensive, she could not wholly rid herself of the feeling that her punishment was in a measure merited, though it was not justice that had dealt with her.

"Well, that is over," said Maxwell, when they were again by themselves.

"Yes, forever," sighed Louise, and for once she was not let have the last word.

"I hope you'll remember that I didn't want to go."

At least, they had not misunderstood each other about Mrs. Harley.

Towards the end of the month, Louise's father and mother came on from Boston. They professed that they had been taken with that wish to see the autumn exhibition at the National Academy which sometimes affects Bostonians, and that their visit had nothing to do with the little hurt that Louise wrote them of when she was quite well of it. They drove over from their hotel the morning they arrived, and she did not know anything of their coming till she heard their voices at the door; her father's voice was rather husky from the climb to her apartment.

The apartment was looking somewhat frouzy, for the Maxwells breakfasted late, and the house-maid had not had time to put it in order. Louise saw it through her father's and mother's eyes with the glance they gave it, and found the rooms ridiculously little, and furnished with cheap Fourteenth Street things; but she bragged all the more noisily of it on that account, and made her mother look out of the window for the pretty view they had from their corner room. Mrs. Hilary pulled her head back from the prospect of the railroad-ridden avenue with silent horror, and Louise burst into a wild laugh. "Well, it *isn't* Commonwealth Avenue, mamma; I don't pretend that, you know."

"Where's Maxwell?" asked Hilary, still puffing from the lounge he had sunk upon as soon as he got into the room.

"Oh, he's down town interviewing a manager about his play."

"I thought that fellow out West had his play. Or is this a new one?"

"No," said Louise, very slowly and thoughtfully, "Brice has taken back his play from Mr. Godolphin." This was true; he *had* taken it back in a sense. She added, as much to herself as to her father, "But he *has* got a new play—that he's working at."

"I hope he hasn't been rash with Godolphin; though I always had an idea that it would have been better for him to deal with a manager. It seems more business-like."

"Oh, much," said Louise.

After a little while they were more at home with each other;

she began to feel herself more their child, and less Maxwell's wife; the barriers of reluctance against him, which she always knew were up with them, fell away from between them and herself. But her father said they had come to get her and Maxwell to lunch with them at their hotel, and then Louise felt herself on her husband's side of the fence again. She said no, they must stay with her; that she was sure Brice would be back for lunch; and she wanted to show them her house-keeping. Mrs. Hilary cast her eye about the room at the word, as if she had seen quite enough of it already, and this made Louise laugh again. She was no better in person than the room was, and she felt her mother's tacit censure apply to her slatternly dressing-gown.

"I know what you're thinking, mamma. But I got the habit of it when I had my strained ankle."

"Oh, I'm sure it must be very comfortable," Mrs. Hilary said, of the dressing-gown. "Is it entirely well now?" she added, of the ankle; and she and Hilary both looked at Louise in a way that would have convinced her that their final anxiety concerning it had brought them to New York, if she had not guessed it already. "The doctor," and by this she meant their old family doctor, as if he were the only one, "said you couldn't be too careful."

"Well, I haven't been careful," said Louise, gayly; "but I'm quite well, and you can go back at once, if that's all, mamma."

Hilary laughed with her. "You haven't changed much, Louise."

Her mother said, in another sense, "I think you look a little pulled down," and that made her and her father laugh again. She got to playing with him, and poking him, and kissing

W. D. Howells

him, in the way she had with him when she was a girl; it was not so very long ago.

Her mother bore with this for awhile, and then she rose to go.

"You're not going to stay!" Louise protested.

"Not to-day, my dear. I've got some shopping to do before lunch."

"Well," said Louise, "I didn't suppose you would stay the first time, such swells as you and papa. But I shall insist upon your coming to-morrow when you've recovered a little from the blow this home of virtuous poverty has given you, and I've had a chance to dust and prepare for you. And I'll tell you what, mamma; Brice and I will come to dinner with you to-night, and we won't take any refusal. We'll be with you at seven. How will that do, papa?"

"That will do," said Hilary, with his arm round her waist, and they kissed each other to clinch the bargain.

"And don't you two old things go away and put your frosty paws together and say Brice and I are not happy. We do quarrel like cats and dogs every now and then, but the rest of the time we're the happiest couple in the universe, and an example to parents."

Hilary would have manifestly liked to stay and have her go on with her nonsense, but his wife took him away.

When Maxwell came in she was so full of their visit that she did not ask him what luck he had with his play, but told him at once they were going to dine with her father and mother. "And I want you to brace up, my dear, and not let them imagine anything."

"How, anything?" he asked, listlessly.

"Oh, nothing. About your play not going perfectly. I didn't think it necessary to go into particulars with them, and you needn't. Just pass it over lightly if they ask you anything about it. But they won't."

Maxwell did not look so happy as he might at the prospect of dining with his wife's father and mother, but he did not say anything disagreeable, and after an instant of silent resentment Louise did not say anything disagreeable either. In fact, she devoted herself to avoiding any displeasures with him, and she arrived with him at the Hilarys' hotel on perfectly good terms, and, as far as he was concerned, in rather good spirits.

Upon the whole, they had a very good time. Hilary made occasion to speak to Maxwell of his letters to the *Abstract*, and told him they were considered by far the best letters of the kind published anywhere, which meant anywhere in Boston.

"You do that sort of thing so well, newspaper writing," he continued, with a slyness that was not lost upon Louise, though Maxwell was ignorant of his drift, "that I wonder you don't sometimes want to take it up again."

"It's well enough," said Maxwell, who was gratified by his praise.

"By the way," said Hilary, "I met your friend, Mr. Ricker, the other day, and he spoke most cordially about you. I fancy he would be very glad to have you back."

"In the old way? I would rather be excused."

"No, from what he said, I thought he would like your writing in the editorial page."

Maxwell looked pleased. "Ricker's always been very good, but he has very little influence on the *Abstract*. He has no money interest in the paper."

Hilary said, with the greatest artfulness, "I wonder he doesn't buy in. I hear it can be done."

"Not by Ricker, for the best of all possible reasons," said Maxwell, with a laugh.

Louise could hardly wait till she had parted from her father and mother before she began on her husband: "You goose! Didn't you see that papa was hinting at buying *you* a share in the *Abstract*?"

"He was very modest about it, then; I didn't see anything of the kind."

"Oh, do you think *you* are the only modest man? Papa is *very* modest, and he wouldn't make you an offer outright, unless he saw that you would like it. But I know that was what he was coming to, and if you'll let me—"

A sentiment of a reluctance rather than a refusal was what made itself perceptible from his arm to hers, as they hurried along the street together, and Louise would not press the question till he spoke again.

He did not speak till they were in the train on their way home. Then he said, "I shouldn't care to have a money interest in a newspaper. It would tie me up to it, and load me down with cares I should hate. It wouldn't be my real life."

"Yes," said his wife, but when they got into their little apartment she cast an eye, opened to its meanness and narrowness, over the common belongings, and wondered if he would ask himself whether this was her real life. But she did not speak, though she was apt to speak out most things that she thought.

XVIII

Some people began to call, old friends of her mother, whose visit to New York seemed to have betrayed to them the fact of Louise's presence for the first time, and some friends of her own, who had married, and come to New York to live, and who said they had just got back to town long enough to learn that she was there. These all reproached her for not having let them know sooner where she was, and they all more or less followed up their reproaches with the invitations which she dreaded because of Maxwell's aversion for them. But she submitted them to him, and submitted to his refusal to go with her, and declined them. In her heart she thought he was rather ungracious, but she did not say so, though in two or three cases of people whom she liked she coaxed him a little to go with her. Meeting her mother and talking over the life she used to lead in Boston, and the life so many people were leading there still, made her a little hungry for society; she would have liked well enough to find herself at a dinner again, and she would have felt a little dancing after the dinner no hardship; but she remembered the promise she had made herself not to tease Maxwell about such things. So she merely coaxed him, and he so far relented as to ask her why she could not go without him, and that hurt her, and she said she never would go without him. All the same, when there came an invitation for lunch, from a particularly nice friend of her girlhood, she hesitated and was lost. She had expected, somehow, that it was going to be a very little lunch, but she found it a very large one, in the number of people, and after the stress of accounting for her husband's failure to come with her, she was not sorry to have it so. She inhaled with joy the atmosphere of the flower-scented rooms; her eye dwelt with delight on their luxurious and tasteful appointments, the belongings of her former life, which seemed to emerge in them from the past and claim her again; the women in their *chic* New York costumes and their miracles of early winter hats hailed her a long-lost sister by every graceful movement and cultivated tone; the correctly tailored and agreeably mannered men had polite intelligence of a world that Maxwell never would and never could be part of; the talk of the little amusing, unvital things that began at once was more precious to her than the problems which the austere imagination of her husband dealt with; it suddenly fatigued her to think how hard she had tried to sympathize with his interest in them. Her heart leaped at sight of the long, rose-heaped table, with its glitter of glass and silver, and the solemn perfection of the serving-men; a spectacle not important in itself was dear to her from association with gayeties, which now, for a wicked moment, seemed to her better than love.

There were all sorts of people: artists and actors, as well as people of fashion. Her friend had given her some society notable to go out with, but she had appointed for the chair next her, on the other hand, a young man in a pretty pointed beard, whom she introduced across from the head of the table as soon as she could civilly take the notable to herself. Louise did not catch his name, and it seemed presently that he had not heard hers, but their acquaintance prospered without this knowledge. He made some little jokes, which she promptly responded to, and they talked awhile as if they were both New-Yorkers, till she said, at some remark of his, "But I am not a New-Yorker," and then he said, "Well,

W. D. Howells

neither am I," and offered to tell her what he was if she would tell him what she was.

"Oh, I'm from Boston, of course," she answered, but then, instead of saying where he was from, he broke out:

"Now I will fulfil my vow!"

"Your vow? What is your vow?"

"To ask the first Boston person I met if that Boston person knew anything about another Boston person, who wrote a most remarkable play I saw in the fall out at home."

"A play?" said Louise, with a total loss of interest in the gentleman's city or country.

"Yes, by a Boston man named Maxwell—"

Louise stared at him, and if their acquaintance had been a little older, she might have asked him to come off. As it was she could not speak, and she let him go on.

"I don't know when I've ever had a stronger impression in the theatre than I had from that play. Perfectly modern, and perfectly American." He briefly sketched it. "It was like a terrible experience on the tragic side, and on the other side it was a rapture. I never saw love-making on the stage before that made me wish to be a lover—"

A fire-red flew over Louise's face, and she said, almost snubbingly, as if he had made some unwarrantable advance: "I think I had better not let you go on. It was my husband who wrote that play. I am Mrs. Maxwell."

"Mrs. Maxwell! You are Mrs. Maxwell?" he gasped, and she

could not doubt the honesty of his amaze.

His confusion was so charming that she instantly relented. "Of course I should like to have you go on all day as you've begun, but there's no telling what exceptions you might be going to make later. Where did you see my husband's play?"

"In Midland—"

"What! You are not—you can't be—Mr. Ray?"

"I am—I can," he returned, gleefully, and now Louise impulsively gave him her hand under the table-cloth.

The man[oe]uvre caught the eye of the hostess. "A bet?" she asked.

"Better," cried Louise, not knowing her pun, "a thousand times," and she turned without further explanation to the gentleman: "When I tell Mr. Maxwell of this he will suffer as he ought, and that's saying a great deal, for not coming with me to-day. To think of it's being *you*!"

"Ah, but to think of it's being *he*! You acquit me of the poor taste of putting up a job?"

"Oh, of anything you want to be acquitted of! What crime would you prefer? There are whole deluges of mercy for you. But now go on, and tell me everything you thought about the play."

"I'd rather you'd tell me what you know about the playwright."

"Everything, of course, and nothing." She added the last words from a sudden, poignant conviction. "Isn't that the way with the wives of you men of genius?"

"Am I a man of genius?"

"You're literary."

"Oh, literary, yes. But I'm not married."

"You're determined to get out of it, somehow. Tell me about Midland. It has filled such a space in our imagination! You can't think what a comfort and stay you have been to us! But why in Midland? Is it a large place?"

"Would it take such a very big one to hold me? It's the place I brought myself up in, and it's very good to me, and so I live there. I don't think it has any vast intellectual or aesthetic interests, but there are very nice people there, very cultivated, some of them, and very well read. After all, you don't need a great many people; three or four will do."

"And have you always lived there?"

"I lived a year or so in New York, and I manage to get on here some time every winter. The rest of the year Midland is quite enough for me. It's gay at times; there's a good deal going on; and I can write there as well as anywhere, and better than in New York. Then, you know, in a small way I'm a prophet in my own country, perhaps because I was away from it for awhile. It's very pretty. But it's very base of you to make me talk about myself when I'm so anxious to hear about Mr. Maxwell."

"And do you spend all your time writing Ibsen criticisms of Ibsen plays?" Louise pursued against his protest.

"I do some other kind of writing."

"As—"

"Oh, no! I'm not here to interview myself."

"Oh, but you ought. I know you've written something—some novel. Your name was so familiar from the first." Mr. Ray laughed and shook his head in mockery of her cheap device. "You mustn't be vexed because I'm so vague about it. I'm very ignorant."

"You said you were from Boston."

"But there are Bostons and Bostons. The Boston that I belonged to never hears of American books till they are forgotten!"

"Ah, how famous I must be there!"

"I see you are determined to be bad. But I remember now; it was a play. Haven't you written a play?" He held up three fingers. "I knew it! What was it?"

"My plays," said the young fellow, with a mock of superiority, "have never been played. I've been told that they are above the heads of an audience. It's a great consolation. But now, really, about Mr. Maxwell's. When is it to be given here? I hoped very much that I might happen on the very time."

Louise hesitated a moment, and then she said: "You know he has taken it back from Godolphin." It was not so hard to say this as it was at first, but it still required resolution.

"Oh, I'm so glad!" said Mr. Ray. "I never thought he appreciated it. He was so anxious to make his part all in all that he would have been willing to damage the rest of it irretrievably. I could see, from the way he talked of it, that he was mortally jealous of Salome; and the girl who did that did it very sweetly and prettily. Who has got the play now?"

"Well," said Louise, with rather a painful smile, "nobody has it at present. We're trying to stir up strife for it among managers."

"What play is that?" asked her friend, the hostess, and all that end of the table became attentive, as any fashionable company will at the mention of a play; books may be more or less out of the range of society, but plays never at all.

"My husband's," said Louise, meekly.

"Why, does *your* husband write *plays*?" cried the lady.

"What did you think he did?" returned Louise, resentfully; she did not in the least know what her friend's husband did, and he was no more there to speak for himself than her own.

"He's written a very *great* play," Mr. Ray spoke up with generous courage; "the very greatest American play I have seen. I don't say ever written, for I've written some myself that I haven't seen yet," he added, and every one laughed at his bit of self-sacrifice. "But Mr. Maxwell's play is just such a play as I would have written if I could—large, and serious, and charming."

He went on about it finely, and Louise's heart swelled with pride. She wished Maxwell could have been there, but if he had been, of course Mr. Ray would not have spoken so freely.

The hostess asked him where he had seen it, and he said in Midland.

Then she said, "We must all go," and she had the effect of rising to do so, but it was only to leave the men to their tobacco.

Louise laid hold of her in the drawing-room: "Who is he? What is he?"

"A little dear, isn't he?"

"Yes, of course. But what has he done?"

"Why, he wrote a novel—I forget the name, but I have it somewhere. It made a great sensation. But surely *you* must know what it was?"

"No, no," Louise lamented. "I am ashamed to say I don't."

When the men joined the ladies, she lingered long enough to thank Mr. Ray, and try to make him tell her the name of his novel. She at least made him promise to let them know the next time he was in New York, and she believed all he said of his regret that he was going home that night. He sent many sweet messages to Maxwell, whom he wanted to talk with about his play, and tell him all he had thought about it. He felt sure that some manager would take it and bring it out in New York, and again he exulted that it was out of the actor's hands. A manager might not have an artistic interest in it; an actor could only have a personal interest in it.

XIX

Louise came home in high spirits. The world seemed to have begun to move again. It was full of all sorts of gay hopes, or at least she was, and she was impatient to impart them to Maxwell. Now she decided that her great office in his life must be to cheer him up, to supply that spring of joyousness which was so lacking in him, and which he never could do any sort of work without. She meant to make him go into society with her. It would do him good, and he would shine. He could talk as well as Mr. Ray, and if he would let himself go, he could be as charming.

She rushed in to speak with him, and was vexed to find a strange man sitting in the parlor alone. The stranger rose at her onset, and then, when she confusedly retreated, he sank into his chair again. She had seen him black against the window, and had not made out any feature or expression of his face.

The maid explained that it was a gentleman who had called to see Mr. Maxwell earlier in the day, and the last time had asked if he might sit down and wait for him. He had been waiting only a few minutes.

"But who is he?" demanded Louise, with a provisional indignation in case it should be a liberty on some unauthorized person's part. "Didn't he give you a card?"

He had given the girl a card, and she now gave it to Mrs. Maxwell. It bore the name Mr. Lawrence Sterne, which Louise read with much the same emotion as if it had been Mr. William Shakespeare. She suspected what her husband would have called a fake of some sort, and she felt a little afraid. She did not like the notion of the man's sitting there in her parlor while she had nobody with her but the girl. He might be all right, and he might even be a gentleman, but the dark bulk which had risen up against the window and stood holding a hat in its hand was not somehow a gentlemanly bulk, the hat was not definitively a gentleman's hat, and the baldness which had shone against the light was not exactly what you would have called a gentleman's baldness. Clearly, however, the only thing to do was to treat the event as one of entire fitness till it proved itself otherwise, and Louise returned to the parlor with an air of lady-*like inquiry, expressed in her look and movement; if this effect was not wholly unmixed with patronage, it still was kind.

"I am sorry," she said, "that my husband is out, and I am sorry to say that I don't know just when he will be at home." She stood and the man had risen again, with his portly frame and his invisible face between her and the light again. "If I could be of any use in giving him a message—" She stopped; it was really sending the man out of the house, and she could not do that; it was not decent. She added, "Or if you don't mind waiting a few minutes longer—"

She sat down, but the man did not. He said: "I can't wait any longer just now; but if Mr. Maxwell would like to see me, I am at the Coleman House." She looked at him as if she did not understand, and he went on: "If he doesn't recall my name he'll remember answering my advertisement, some weeks ago in the *Theatrical Register*, for a play."

W. D. Howells

"Oh yes!" said Louise. This was the actor whom she had written to on behalf of Maxwell. With electrical suddenness and distinctness she now recalled the name, L. Sterne, along with all the rest, though the card of Mr. Lawrence Sterne had not stirred her sleeping consciousness. She had always meant to tell Maxwell what she had done, but she was always waiting for something to come of it, and when nothing came of it, she did not tell; she had been so disgusted at the mere notion of answering the man's advertisement. Now, here was the man himself, and he had to be answered, and that would probably be worse than answering his advertisement. "I remember," she said, provisionally, but with the resolution to speak exactly the truth; "I wrote to you *for* Mr. Maxwell," which did not satisfy her as the truth ought to have done.

"Well, then, I wish you would please tell him that I didn't reply to his letter because it kept following me from place to place, and I only got it at the *Register* office this morning."

"I will tell Mr. Maxwell," said Louise.

"I should be glad to see his play, if he still has it to dispose of. From what Mr. Grayson has told me of it, I think it might—I think I should like to see it. It might suit the—the party I am acting for," he added, letting himself go.

"Then you are not the—the—star?"

"I am the manager for the star."

"Oh," said Louise, with relief. The fact seemed to put another complexion on the affair. A distaste which she had formed for Mr. Sterne personally began to cede to other feelings. If he was manager for the star, he must be like other managers, such as Maxwell was willing to deal with, and if he knew Mr. Grayson he must be all right. "I will tell Mr. Maxwell," she said, with no provisionality this time.

Mr. Sterne prepared to go, so far as buttoning his overcoat and making some paces towards the door gave token of his intention. Louise followed him with a politeness which was almost gratitude to him for reinstating her in her own esteem. He seemed to have atmospheric intelligence of her better will towards him, for he said, as if it were something she might feel an interest in: "If I can get a play that will suit, I shall take the road with a combination immediately after New Year's. I don't know whether you have ever seen the lady I want the play for."

"The lady?" gasped Louise.

"She isn't very well-known in the East yet, but she will be. She wants a play of her own. As I understand Mr. Grayson, there is a part in Mr. Maxwell's play that would fit her to a T, or could be fitted to her; these things always need some little adaptation." Mr. Sterne's manner became easier and easier. "Curious thing about it is that you are next door—or next floor—neighbors, here. Mrs. Harley."

"We—we have met her," said Louise in a hollow murmur.

"Well, you can't have any idea what Yolande Havisham is from Mrs. Harley. I shall be at the Coleman the whole evening, if Mr. Maxwell would like to call. Well, good-morning," said Mr. Sterne, and he got himself away before Louise could tell him that Maxwell would never give his play to a woman; before she could say that it was already as good as accepted by another manager; before she could declare that if no manager ever wanted it, still, as far as Mrs. Harley was concerned, with her smouldering eyes, it would always be in negotiation; before she could form or express any utter and final refusal and denial of his abominable hopes.

It remained for her either to walk quietly down to the North River and drown herself or to wait her husband's return and tell him everything and throw herself on his mercy, implore him, adjure him, not to give that woman his play; and then to go into a decline that would soon rid him of the clog and hinderance she had always been to him. It flashed through her turmoil of emotion that it was already dark, in spite of Mr. Sterne's good-morning at parting, and that some one might speak to her on the way to the river; and then she thought how Maxwell would laugh when she told him the fear of being spoken to had kept her from suicide; and she sat waiting for him to come with such an inward haggardness that she was astonished, at sight of herself in the glass, to find that she wan looking very much as usual. Maxwell certainly noticed no difference when he came in and flung himself wearily on the lounge, and made no attempt to break the silence of their meeting; they had kissed, of course, but had not spoken.

She was by no means sure what she was going to do; she had hoped there would be some leading on his part that would make it easy for her to do right, whatever the right was, but her heart sank at sight of him. He looked defeated and harassed. But there was no help for it. She must speak, and speak unaided; the only question was whether she had better speak before dinner or after. She decided to speak after dinner, and then all at once she was saying: "Brice, I have brought something dreadful on myself."

"At the lunch?" he asked, wearily, and she saw that he thought she had been making some silly speech she was ashamed of.

"Oh, if it had only been at the lunch!" she cried. "No, it was here—here in this very room."

"*I* don't know what's the matter with you, Louise," he said, lying back and shutting his eyes.

"Then I must tell you!" And she came out with the whole story, which she had to repeat in parts before he could understand it. When he did understand that she had answered an advertisement in the *Register*, in his name, he opened his eyes and sat up.

"Well?" he said.

"Well, don't you see how wrong and wicked that was?"

"I've heard of worse things."

"Oh, don't say so, dearest! It was living a lie, don't you see. And I've been living a lie ever since, and now I'm justly punished for not telling you long ago."

She told him of the visit she had just had, and who the man was, and whom he wanted the play for; and now a strange thing happened with her. She did not beseech him not to give his play to that woman; on the contrary she said: "And now, Brice, I want you to let her have it. I know she will play Salome magnificently, and that will make the fortune of the piece, and it will give you such a name that anything you write after this will get accepted; and you can satisfy your utmost ambition, and you needn't mind me—no—or think of me at all any more than if I were the dust of the earth; and I am! Will you?"

He got up from the lounge and began to walk the floor, as he always did when he was perplexed; and she let him walk up and down in silence as long as she could bear it. At last she said: "I am in earnest, Brice, I am indeed, and if you don't do it, if you let me or my feelings stand in your way, in the slightest degree, I will never forgive you. Will you go straight down to the Coleman House, as soon as you've had your dinner, and tell that man he can have your play for that woman?"

"No," said Maxwell, stopping in his walk, and looking at her in a dazed way.

Her heart seemed to leap into her throat. "Why?" she choked.

"Because Godolphin is here."

"Godo—" she began; and she cast herself on the lounge that Maxwell had vacated, and plunged her face in the pillow and sobbed, "Oh, cruel, cruel, *cruel*! Oh, *cruel*, cruel, cruel, cruel!"

XX

Maxwell stood looking at his wife with the cold disgust which hysterics are apt to inspire in men after they have seen them more than once. "I suppose that when you are ready you will tell me what is the matter with you."

"To let me suffer so, when you knew all the time that Godolphin was here, and you needn't give your play to that creature at all," wailed Louise.

"How did *I* know you were suffering?" he retorted. "And how do I know that I can do anything with Godolphin?"

"Oh, I *know* you can!" She sprang up with the greatest energy, and ran into the bedroom to put in order her tumbled hair; she kept talking to him from there. "I want you to go down and see him the instant you have had dinner; and don't let him escape you. Tell him he can have the play on any terms. I believe he is the only one who can make it go. He was the first to appreciate the idea, and—Frida!" she called into the hall towards the kitchen, "we will have dinner at once, now, please—he always talked so intelligently about it; and now if he's where you can superintend the rehearsals, it will be the greatest success. How in the world did you find out he was here?"

She came out of her room, in surprising repair, with this question, and the rest of their talk went on through dinner.

It appeared that Maxwell had heard of Godolphin's presence from Grayson, whom he met in the street, and who told him that Godolphin had made a complete failure of his venture. His combination had gone to pieces at Cleveland, and his company were straggling back to New York as they could. Godolphin was deeply in debt to them all, and to everybody else; and yet the manager spoke cordially of him, and with no sort of disrespect, as if his insolvency were only an affair of the moment, which he would put right. Louise took the same view of it, and she urged Maxwell to consider how Godolphin had promptly paid him, and would always do so.

"Probably I got the pay of some poor devil who needed it worse," said Maxwell.

She said, "Nonsense! The other actors will take care of all that. They are so good to each other," and she blamed Maxwell for not going to see Godolphin at once.

"That was what I did," he answered, "but he wasn't at home. He was to be at home after dinner."

"Well, that makes it all the more providential," said Louise; her piety always awoke in view of favorable chances. "You mustn't lose any time. Better not wait for the coffee."

"I think I'll wait for the coffee," said Maxwell. "It's no use going there before eight."

"No," she consented. "Where is he stopping?"

"At the Coleman House."

"The Coleman House? Then if that wretch should see you?" She meant the manager of Mrs. Harley.

"He wouldn't know me, probably," Maxwell returned, scornfully. "But if you think there's any danger of his laying hold of me, and getting the play away before Godolphin has a chance of refusing it, I'll go masked. I'm tired of thinking about it. What sort of lunch did you have?"

"I had the best time in the world. You ought to have come with me, Brice. I shall make you, the next one. Oh, and guess who was there! Mr. Ray!"

"*Our* Mr. Ray?" Maxwell breathlessly demanded.

"There is no other, and he's the sweetest little dear in the world. He isn't so big as you are, even, and he's such a merry spirit; he hasn't the bulk your gloom gives you. I want you to be like him, Brice. I don't see why you shouldn't go into society, too."

"If I'd gone into society to-day, I should have missed seeing Grayson, and shouldn't have known Godolphin was in town."

"Well, that is true, of course. But if you get your play into Godolphin's hands, you'll have to show yourself a little, so that nice people will be interested in it. You ought to have heard Mr. Ray celebrate it. He piped up before the whole table."

Louise remembered what Ray said very well, and she repeated it to a profound joy in Maxwell. It gave him an exquisite pleasure, and it flattered him to believe that, as the hostess had said in response, they, the nice people, must see it, though he had his opinion of nice people, apart from their usefulness in seeing his play. To reward his wife for it all, he rose as soon as he had drunk his coffee, and went out to put on his hat and coat. She went with him, and saw that he put them on properly, and did not go off with half his coat-collar turned up. After he got his hat on, she took it off to see whether his cow-lick was worse than usual.

"Why, good heavens! Godolphin's seen me before, and besides, I'm not going to propose marriage to him," he protested.

"Oh, it's much more serious than that!" she sighed. "Anybody would take *you*, dear, but it's your play we want him to take—or take back."

When Maxwell reached the hotel, he did not find Godolphin there. He came back twice; then, as something in his manner seemed to give Maxwell authority, the clerk volunteered to say that he thought he might find the actor at the Players' Club. In this hope he walked across to Gramercy Park. Godolphin had been dining there, and when he got Maxwell's name, he came half way down the stairs to meet him. He put his arm round him to return to the library.

There happened to be no one else there, and he made Maxwell sit down in an arm-chair fronting his own, and give an account of himself since they parted. He asked after Mrs. Maxwell's health, and as far as Maxwell could make out he was sincere in the quest. He did not stop till he had asked, with the most winning and radiant smile, "And the play, what have you done with the play?"

He was so buoyant that Maxwell could not be heavy about it, and he answered as gayly: "Oh, I fancy I have been waiting for you to come on and take it."

Godolphin did not become serious, but he became if possible

more sincere. "Do you really think I could do anything with it?"

"If you can't nobody can."

"Why, that is very good of you, very good indeed, Maxwell. Do you know, I have been thinking about that play. You see, the trouble was with the Salome. The girl I had for the part was a thoroughly nice girl, but she hadn't the weight for it. She did the comic touches charmingly, but when it came to the tragedy she wasn't there. I never had any doubt that I could create the part of Haxard. It's a noble part. It's the greatest role on the modern stage. It went magnificently in Chicago—with the best people. You saw what the critics said of it?"

"No; you didn't send me the Chicago papers." Maxwell did not say that all this was wholly different from what Godolphin had written him when he renounced the play. Yet he felt that Godolphin was honest then and was honest now. It was another point of view; that was all.

"Ah, I thought I sent them. There was some adverse criticism of the play as a whole, but there was only one opinion of Haxard. And you haven't done anything with the piece yet?"

"No, nothing."

"And you think I could do Haxard? You still have faith in me?"

"As much faith as I ever had," said Maxwell; and Godolphin found nothing ambiguous in a thing certainly susceptible of two interpretations.

"That is very good of you, Maxwell; very good." He lifted

W. D. Howells

his fine head and gazed absently a moment at the wall before him. "Well, then I will tell you what I will do, Mr. Maxwell; I will take the play."

"You will!"

"Yes; that is if you think I can do the part."

"Why, of course!"

"And if—if there could be some changes—very slight changes—made in the part of Salome. It needs subduing." Godolphin said this as if he had never suggested anything of the kind before; as if the notion were newly evolved from his experience.

"I will do what I can, Mr. Godolphin," Maxwell promised, while he knitted his brows in perplexity "But I do think that the very strength of Salome gives relief to Haxard—gives him greater importance."

"It *may* be so, dramatically. But theatrically, it detracts from him. Haxard must be the central figure in the eye of the audience from first to last."

Maxwell mused for a moment of discouragement. They were always coming back to that; very likely Godolphin was right; but Maxwell did not know just how to subdue the character of Salome so as to make her less interesting. "Do you think that was what gave you bad houses in Chicago—the double interest, or the weakened interest in Haxard?"

"I think so," said Godolphin.

"Were the houses bad—comparatively?"

Godolphin took a little note-book out of his breast-pocket. "Here are my dates. I opened the first night, the tenth of November, with Haxard, but we papered the house thoroughly, and we made a good show to the public and the press. There were four hundred and fifty dollars in it. The next night there were three hundred; the next night, two eighty; Wednesday matinee, less than two hundred. That night we put on 'Virginius,' and played to eight hundred dollars; Thursday night, with the 'Lady of Lyons,' we had eleven hundred; Friday night, we gave the 'Lady' to twelve hundred; Saturday afternoon with the same piece, we took in eleven hundred and fifty; Saturday night, with 'Ingomar,' we had fifteen hundred dollars in the house, and a hundred people standing." Maxwell listened with a drooping head; he was bitterly mortified. "But it was too late then," said Godolphin, with a sigh, as he shut his hook.

"Do you mean," demanded Maxwell, "that my piece had crippled you so that—that—"

"I didn't say that, Mr. Maxwell. I never meant to let you see the figures. But you asked me."

"Oh, you're quite right," said Maxwell. He thought how he had blamed the actor, in his impatience with him, for not playing his piece oftener—and called him fool and thought him knave for not doing it all the time, as Godolphin had so lavishly promised to do. He caught at a straw to save himself from sinking with shame. "But the houses, were they so bad everywhere?"

Godolphin checked himself in a movement to take out his note-book again; Maxwell had given him such an imploring glance. "They were pretty poor everywhere. But it's been a bad season with a good many people."

"No, no," cried Maxwell. "You did very well with the other plays, Godolphin. Why do you want to touch the thing again? It's been ruinous to you so far. Give it up! Come! I can't let you have it!"

Godolphin laughed, and all his beautiful white teeth shone. There was a rich, wholesome red in his smoothly shaven cheeks; he was a real pleasure to the eye. "I believe it would go better in New York. I'm not afraid to try it. You mustn't take away my last chance of retrieving the season. Hair of the dog, you know. Have you seen Grayson lately?"

"Yes, I saw him this afternoon. It was he that told me you were in town."

"Ah, yes."

"And Godolphin, I've got it on my conscience, if you do take the play, to tell you that I offered it to Grayson, and he refused it. I think you ought to know that; it's only fair; and for the matter of that, it's been kicking round all the theatres in New York."

"Dear boy!" said Godolphin, caressingly, and with a smile that was like a benediction, "that doesn't make the least difference."

"Well, I wished you to know," said Maxwell, with a great load off his mind.

"Yes, I understand that. Will you drink anything, or smoke anything? Or—I forgot! I hate all that, too. But you'll join me in a cup of tea downstairs?" They descended to the smoking-room below, and Godolphin ordered the tea, and went on talking with a gay irrelevance till it came. Then he said, as he poured out the two cups of it: "The fact is, Grayson is going in with me, if I do your piece." This was news to Maxwell, and yet he was somehow not surprised at it. "I dare say he told you?"

"No, he didn't give me any hint of it. He simply told me that you were in town, and where you were."

"Ah, that was like Grayson. Queer fish."

"But I'm mighty glad to know it. You can make it go, together, if any power on earth can do it; and if it fails," Maxwell added, "I shall have the satisfaction of ruining some one else this time."

"Well, Grayson has made nearly as bad a mess of it as I have, this season," said Godolphin. "He's got to take off that thing he has going now, and it's a question of what he shall put on. It will be an experiment with Haxard, but I believe it will be a successful experiment. I have every confidence in that play." Godolphin looked up, his lips set convincingly, and with the air of a man who had stood unfalteringly by his opinion from the first. "Now, if you will excuse me, I will tell you what I think ought to be done to it."

"By all means," said Maxwell; "I shall be glad to do anything you wish, or that I can."

Godolphin poured out a cloudy volume of suggestion, with nothing clear in it but the belief that the part of Haxard ought to be fattened. He recurred to all the structural impossibilities that he had ever desired, and there was hardly a point in the piece that he did not want changed. At the end he said: "But all these things are of no consequence, comparatively speaking. What we need is a woman who can take the part of Salome, and play it with all the feminine charm that you've given it, and yet keep it strictly in the background, or thoroughly subordinated to the interest of Haxard."

For all that Godolphin seemed to have learned from his experience with the play, Maxwell might well have thought they were still talking of it at Magnolia. It was a great relief to his prepossessions in the form of conclusions to have Grayson appear, with the air of looking for some one, and of finding the object of his search in Godolphin. He said he was glad to see Maxwell, too, and they went on talking of the play. From the talk of the other two Maxwell perceived that the purpose of doing his play had already gone far with them; but they still spoke of it as something that would be very good if the interest could be unified in it. Suddenly the manager broke out: "Look here, Godolphin! I have an idea! Why not frankly accept the inevitable! I don't believe Mr. Maxwell can make the play different from what it is, structurally, and I don't believe the character of Salome can be subdued or subordinated. Then why not play Salome as strongly as possible, and trust to her strength to enhance Haxard's effect, instead of weakening it?"

Godolphin smiled towards Maxwell: "That was your idea."

"Yes," said Maxwell, and he kept himself from falling on Grayson's neck for joy.

"It might do," the actor assented with smiling eagerness and tolerant superiority. "But whom could you get for such a Salome as that?"

"Well, there's only one woman for it," said Grayson.

"Yolande Havisham?"

The name made Maxwell's heart stop. He started forward to say that Mrs. Harley could not have the part, when the manager said: "And we couldn't get her. Sterne has engaged her to star in his combination. By the way, he was looking for you to-day, Mr. Maxwell."

"I missed him," answered Maxwell, with immense relief. "But I should not have let him have the piece while I had the slightest hope of your taking it."

Neither the manager nor the actor was perhaps greatly moved by his generous preference, though they both politely professed to be so. They went on to canvass the qualities and reputations of all the other actresses attainable, and always came back to Yolande Havisham, who was unattainable; Sterne would never give her up in the world, even if she were willing to give up the chance he was offering her. But she was the one woman who could do Salome.

They decided that they must try to get Miss Pettrell, who had played the part with Godolphin, and who had done it with refinement, if not with any great force. When they had talked to this conclusion, Grayson proposed getting something to eat, and the others refused, but they went into the dining-room with him, where he showed Maxwell the tankards of the members hanging on the walls over their tables—Booth's tankard, Salvini's, Irving's, Jefferson's. He was surprised that Maxwell was not a member of the Players, and said that he must be; it was the only club for him, if he was going to write for the stage. He came out with them and pointed out several artists whose fame Maxwell knew, and half a dozen literary men, among them certain playwrights; they were all smoking, and the place was blue with the fumes of their cigars. The actors were coming in from the theatres for supper, and Maxwell found himself with his friends in a group with a charming old comedian who was telling brief, vivid little stories, and sketching character, with illustrations from his delightful art. He was not swagger, like some of the

W. D. Howells

younger men who stood about with their bell-crowned hats on, before they went into supper; and two or three other elderly actors who sat round him and took their turn in the anecdote and mimicry looked, with their smooth-shaven faces, like old-fashioned ministers. Godolphin, who was like a youthful priest, began to tell stories, too; and he told very good ones admirably, but without appearing to feel their quality, though he laughed loudly at them with the rest.

When Maxwell refused every one's wish to have him eat or drink something, and said good-night, Grayson had already gone in to his supper, and Godolphin rose and smiled so fondly upon him that Maxwell felt as if the actor had blessed him. But he was less sure than in the beginning of the evening that the play was again in Godolphin's hands; and he had to confirm himself from his wife's acceptance of the facts in the belief that it was really so.

XXI

Louise asked Maxwell, as soon as they had established their joint faith, whom Godolphin was going to get to play Salome, and he said that Grayson would like to re-engage Miss Pettrell, though he had a theory that the piece would be strengthened, and the effect of Haxard enhanced, if they could have a more powerful Salome.

"Mr. Ray told me at lunch," said Louise, impartially but with an air of relief, "that in all the love-making she was delightful; but when it came to the tragedy, she wasn't there."

"Grayson seemed to think that if she could be properly rehearsed, she could be brought up to it," Maxwell interposed.

"Mr. Ray said she was certainly very refined, and her Salome was always a lady. And that is the essential thing," Louise added, decisively. "I don't at all agree with Mr. Grayson about having Salome played so powerfully. I think Mr. Godolphin is right."

"For Heaven's sake don't tell him so!" said Maxwell. "We have had trouble enough to get him under."

"Indeed, I shall tell him so! I think he ought to know how

W. D. Howells

we feel."

"*We?*" repeated Maxwell.

"Yes. What we want for Salome is sweetness and delicacy and refinement; for she has to do rather a bold thing, and yet keep herself a lady."

"Well, it may be too late to talk of Miss Pettrell now," said Maxwell. "Your favorite Godolphin parted enemies with her."

"Oh, stage enemies! Mr. Grayson can get her, and he must."

"I'll tell him what your orders are," said Maxwell.

The next day he saw the manager, but nothing had been done, and the affair seemed to be hanging fire again. In the evening, while he was talking it over with his wife in a discouragement which they could not shake off, a messenger came to him with a letter from the Argosy Theatre, which he tore nervously open.

"What is it, dear?" asked his wife, tenderly. "Another disappointment?"

"Not exactly," he returned, with a husky voice, and after a moment of faltering he gave her the letter. It was from Grayson, and it was to the effect that he had seen Sterne, and that Sterne had agreed to a proposition he had made him, to take Maxwell's play on the road, if it succeeded, and in view of this had agreed to let Yolande Havisham take the part of Salome.

Godolphin was going to get all his old company together as far as possible, with the exception of Miss Pettrell, and there was to be little or no delay, because the actors had mostly got back to New York, and were ready to renew their engagements. That no time might be lost, Grayson asked Maxwell to come the next morning and read the piece to such of them as he could get together in the Argosy greenroom, and give them his sense of it.

Louise handed him back the letter, and said, with dangerous calm: "You might save still more time by going down to Mrs. Harley's apartment and reading it to her at once." Maxwell was miserably silent, and she pursued: "May I ask whether you knew they were going to try to get her?"

"No," said Maxwell.

"Was there anything said about her?"

"Yes, there was, last night. But both Grayson and Godolphin regarded it as impossible to get her."

"Why didn't you tell me that they would like to get her?"

"You knew it, already. And I thought, as they both had given up the hope of getting her, I wouldn't mention the subject. It's always been a very disagreeable one."

"Yes." Louise sat quiet, and then she said: "What a long misery your play has been to me!"

"You haven't helped make it any great joy to me," said Maxwell, bitterly.

She began to weep, silently, and he stood looking down at her in utter wretchedness. "Well," he said at last, "what shall I do about it?"

Louise wiped her tears, and cleared up cold, as we say of the weather. She rose, as if to leave the room, and said, haughtily: "You shall do as you think best for yourself. You must let them have the play, and let them choose whom they think best for the part. But you can't expect me to come to see it."

"Then that unsays all the rest. If you don't come to see it, I sha'n't, and I shall not let them have the piece. That is all. Louise," he entreated, after these first desperate words, "*can't* we grapple with this infernal nightmare, so as to get it into the light, somehow, and see what it really is? How can it matter to you who plays the part? Why do you care whether Miss Pettrell or Mrs. Harley does it?"

"Why do you ask such a thing as that?" she returned, in the same hard frost. "You know where the idea of the character came from, and why it was sacred to me. Or perhaps you forget!"

"No, I don't forget. But try—can't you try?—to specify just why you object to Mrs. Harley?"

"You have your theory. You said I was jealous of her."

"I didn't mean it. I never believed that."

"Then I can't explain. If you don't understand, after all that's been said, what is the use of talking? I'm tired of it!"

She went into her room, and he sank into the chair before his desk and sat there, thinking. When she came back, after a while, he did not look round at her, and she spoke to the back of his head. "Should you have any objection to my going home for a few days?"

"No," he returned.

"I know papa would like to have me, and I think you would be less hampered in what you will have to do now if I'm not here."

"You're very considerate. But if that's what you are going for, you might as well stay. I'm not going to do anything whatever."

"Now, you mustn't talk foolishly, Brice," she said, with an air of superior virtue mixed with a hint of martyrdom. "I won't have you doing anything rash or boyish. You will go on and let them have your play just the same as if I didn't exist." She somewhat marred the effect of her self-devotion by adding: "And I shall go on just as if *it* didn't exist." He said nothing, and she continued: "You couldn't expect me to take any interest in it after this, could you? Because, though I am ready to make any sort of sacrifice for you, I think any one, I don't care who it was, would say that was a little *too* much. Don't you think so yourself?"

"You are always right. I think that."

"Don't be silly. I am trying to do the best I can, and you have no right to make it hard for me."

Maxwell wheeled round in his chair: "Then I wish you wouldn't make your best so confoundedly disagreeable."

"Oh!" she twitted. "I see that you have made up your mind to let them have the play, after all."

"Yes, I have," he answered, savagely.

"Perhaps you meant to do it all along?"

"Perhaps I did."

"Very well, then," said Louise. "Would you mind coming to the train with me on your way down town to-morrow?"

"Not at all."

XXII

In the morning neither of them recurred to what Louise had said of her going home for a few days. She had apparently made no preparation for the journey; but if she was better than her words in this, he was quite as bad as his in going down town after breakfast to let Grayson have the play, no matter whom he should get to do Salome. He did not reiterate his purpose, but she knew from the sullen leave, or no-leave, which he took of her, that it was fixed.

When he was gone she had what seemed to her the very worst quarter of an hour she had ever known; but when he came back in the afternoon, looking haggard but savage, her ordeal had long been over. She asked him quietly if they had come to any definite conclusion about the play, and he answered, with harsh aggression, yes, that Mrs. Harley had agreed to take the part of Salome; Godolphin's old company had been mostly got together, and they were to have the first rehearsal the next morning.

"Should you like me to come some time?" asked Louise.

"I should like you very much to come," said Maxwell, soberly, but with a latent doubt of her meaning, which she perceived.

"I have been thinking," she said, "whether you would like me to call on Mrs. Harley this evening with you?"

"What for?" he demanded, suspiciously.

"Well, I don't know. I thought it might be appropriate."

Maxwell thought a moment. "I don't think it would be expected. After all, it isn't a personal thing," he said, with a relenting in his defiance.

"No," said Louise.

They got through the evening without further question.

They had always had some sort of explicit making-up before, even when they had only had a tacit falling out, but this time Louise thought there had better be none of that. They were to rehearse the play every day that week, and Maxwell said he must be at the theatre the next morning at eleven. He could not make out to his wife's satisfaction that he was of much use, but he did not try to convince her. He only said that they referred things to him now and then, and that generally he did not seem to know much about them. She saw that his aesthetic honesty kept him from pretending to more than this, and she believed he ought to have greater credit than he claimed.

Four or five days later she went with him to a rehearsal. By this time they had got so well forward with their work at the theatre that Maxwell said it would now be in appreciable shape; but still he warned her not to expect too much. He never could tell her just what she wanted to know about Mrs. Harley; all he could say was that her Salome was not ideal, though it had strong qualities; and he did not try to keep her from thinking it offensive; that would only have made bad worse.

It had been snowing overnight, and there was a bright glare of sunshine on the drifts, which rendered the theatre doubly dark when they stepped into it from the street. It was a dramatic event for Louise to enter by the stage-door, and to find Maxwell recognized by the old man in charge as having authority to do so; and she made as much of the strange interior as the obscurity and her preoccupation would allow. There was that immediate bareness and roughness which seems the first characteristic of the theatre behind the scenes, where the theatre is one of the simplest and frankest of workshops, in which certain effects are prepared to be felt before the footlights. Nothing of the glamour of the front is possible; there is a hard air of business in everything; and the work that goes to the making of a play shows itself the severest toil. Figures now came and went in the twilight beyond the reach of the gas in the door-keeper's booth, but rapidly as if bent upon definite errands, and with nothing of that loitering gayety which is the imagined temperament of the stage.

Louise and Maxwell were to see Grayson first in his private office, and while their names were taken in, the old door-keeper gave them seats on the Mourners' Bench, a hard wooden settee in the corridor, which he said was the place where actors wanting an engagement waited till the manager sent word that he could see them. The manager did not make the author and his wife wait, but came for them himself, and led the way back to his room. When he gave them seats there, Maxwell had the pleasure of seeing that Louise made an excellent impression with the magnate, of whom he had never quite lost the awe we feel for the master of our fortunes, whoever he is. He perceived that her inalienable worldly splendor added to his own consequence, and that his wife's air of *grande dame* was not lost upon a man who could at least enjoy it artistically. Grayson was very polite to her, and said hopefuller things about the play than he had yet said to Maxwell, though he had always been civil about its merits. He had a number of papers before him, and he asked Louise if she had noticed their friendliness. She said, yes, she had seen some of those things, but she had supposed they were authorized, and she did not know how much to value them.

Grayson laughed and confessed that he did not practice any concealments with the press when it was a question of getting something to the public notice. "Of course," he said, "we don't want the piece to come in on rubbers."

"What do you mean?" she demanded, with an ignorant joy in the phrase.

"That's what we call it when a thing hasn't been sufficiently heralded, or heralded at all. We have got to look after that part of it, you know."

"Of course, I am not complaining, though I think all that's dreadful."

The manager assented partly. Then he said: "There's something curious about it. You may put up the whole affair yourself, and yet in what's said you can tell whether there's a real good will that comes from the writers themselves or not."

"And you mean that there is this mystical kindness for Mr. Maxwell's play in the prophecies that all read so much alike to me?"

"Yes, I do," said the manager, laughing. "They like him because he's new and young, and is making his way single-handed."

"Well," said Louise, "those seem good grounds for preference to me, too;" and she thought how nearly they had been
her own grounds for liking Maxwell.

Grayson went with them to the stage and found her the best
place to sit and see the rehearsal. He made some one get
chairs, and he sat with her chatting while men in high hats
and overcoats and women in bonnets and fur-edged
butterfly-capes came in one after another. Godolphin arrived
among the first, with an ulster which came down to where
his pantaloons were turned up above his overshoes. He
caught sight of Louise, and approached her with outstretched
hand, and Grayson gave up his chair to the actor. Godolphin
was very cordial, deferentially cordial, with a delicate vein of
reminiscent comradery running through his manner. She
spoke to him of having at last got his ideal for Salome, and
he said, with a slight sigh and a sort of melancholy absence:
"Yes, Miss Havisham will do it magnificently." Then he
asked, with a look of latent significance:

"Have you ever seen her?"

Louise laughed for as darkling a reason. "Only in real life.
You know we live just over and under each other."

"Ah, true. But I meant, on the stage. She's a great artist. You
know she's the one I wanted for Salome from the start."

"Then you ought to be very happy in getting her at last."

"She will do everything for the play," sighed Godolphin.
"She'll make up for all my shortcomings."

"You won't persuade us that you have any shortcomings, Mr.

W. D. Howells

Godolphin," said Louise. "You are Haxard, and Haxard is the play. You can't think, Mr. Godolphin, how deeply grateful we both are to you for your confidence in my husband's work, your sacrifices—"

"You overpay me a thousand times for everything, Mrs. Maxwell," said the actor. "Any one might have been proud and happy to do all I've done, and more, for such a play. I've never changed my opinion for a moment that it was *the* American drama. And now if Miss Havisham only turns out to be the Salome we want!"

"If?" returned Louise, and she felt a wild joy in the word. "Why, I thought there could be no earthly doubt about it."

"Oh, there isn't. We are all united on that point, I believe, Maxwell?"

Maxwell shrugged. "I confide in you and Mr. Grayson."

Godolphin looked at his watch. "It's eleven now, and she isn't here yet. I would rather not have begun without her, but I think we had better not delay any longer." He excused himself to Louise, and went and sat down with his hat on at a small table, lit with a single electric bulb, dropping like a luminous spider by a thread from the dark above. Other electric bulbs were grouped before reflectors on either side of the stage, and these shone on the actors before Godolphin. Back in the depths of the stage, some scene-painters and carpenters were at work on large strips of canvas lying unrolled upon the floor or stretched upon light wooden frames. Across Godolphin's head the dim hollow of the auditorium showed, pierced by long bars of sunlight full of dancing motes, which slanted across its gloom from the gallery windows. Women in long aprons were sweeping the floors and pounding the seats, and a smell of dust from their labors mixed with the smell of paint and glue and escaping gas which pervaded the atmosphere of the stage.

Godolphin made Maxwell come and sit with him at the table; he opened his prompt-book and directed the rehearsal to begin. The people were mostly well up in their parts, and the work went smoothly, except for now and then an impatience in Godolphin which did not seem to come from what was going forward.

He showed himself a thorough master of his trade in its more mechanical details, and there were signal instances of his intelligence in the higher things of it which might well have put Mrs. Maxwell to shame for her many hasty judgments of the actor. He was altogether more of a man, more of a mind, than she had supposed, even when she supposed the best of him. She perceived that Godolphin grasped the whole meaning of her husband's work, and interpreted its intentions with perfect accuracy, not only in his own part of Haxard, but in all the other persons, and he corrected the playing of each of the roles as the rehearsal went on. She saw how he had really formed the other actors upon himself. They repeated his tones, his attitudes, his mannerisms, in their several ways. His touch could be felt all through the performance, and his limitations characterized it. He was very gentle and forbearing with their mistakes, but he was absolute master all the same. If some one erred, Godolphin left his place and went and showed how the thing should be said and done. He carefully addressed the men by their surnames, with the Mr. always; the women were all Dear to him, according to a convention of the theatre. He said, "No, dear," and "Yes, dear," and he was as caressingly deferential to each of them as he was formally deferential to the men; he required the same final obedience of them, and it was not always so easy to make them obey. In non-essentials he yielded at times, as when one of the ladies had overdone a

W. D. Howells

point, and he demurred. "But I always got a laugh on that, Mr. Godolphin," she protested. "Oh, well, my dear, hang on to your laugh, then." However he meant to do Haxard himself, his voice was for simplicity and reality in others. "Is that the way you would do it, is that the way you would say it, if it were *you*?" he stopped one of the men in a bit of rant.

Even of Maxwell he exacted as clear a vision of his own work as he exacted of its interpreters. He asked the author his notion of points in dress and person among the different characters, which he had hitherto only generalized in his mind, and which he was gladly willing, when they were brought home to him, to leave altogether to Godolphin's judgment.

The rehearsal had gone well on towards the end of the first act, and Godolphin was beginning to fidget. From where she sat Louise saw him take out his watch and lean towards her husband to say something. An actor who was going through a piece of business perceived that he had not Godolphin's attention, and stopped. Just then Mrs. Harley came in.

Godolphin rose and advanced towards her with the prompt-book shut on his thumb. "You are late, Miss Havisham."

"Yes," she answered, haughtily, as if in resentment of his tone. She added in concession, "Unavoidably. But Salome doesn't come on till the end of the act."

"I think it best for the whole company to be present from the beginning," said Godolphin.

"I quite agree with you," said Mrs. Harley. "Where are we?" she asked, and then she caught sight of Louise, and came up to her. "How do you do, Mrs. Maxwell? I don't know whether I'm glad to see you or not. I believe I'm rather afraid to have you see my Salome; I've an idea you are going to be very severe with her."

"I am sure no severity will be needed. You'll see me nodding approval all the way through," Louise returned.

"I have always thought, somehow, that you had the part especially under your protection. I feel that I'm a very bold woman to attempt it."

In spite of her will to say "Yes, a very bold woman indeed!" Louise answered: "Then I shall admire your courage, as well as your art."

She was aware of Godolphin fretting at the colloquy he could not interrupt, and of Mrs. Harley prolonging it wilfully. "I know you are sincere, and I am going to make you tell me everything you object to in me when it's over. Will you?"

"Of course," Louise answered, gayly; and now Mrs. Harley turned to Godolphin again: "*Where* were you?"

XXIII

Twice during the rehearsal Maxwell came to Louise and asked her if she were not tired and would not like to go home; he offered to go out and put her on a car. But both times she made him the same answer: she was not tired, and would not go away on any account; the second time she said, with a certain meaning in her look and voice, that she thought she could stand it if he could. At the end she went up and made her compliments to Mrs. Harley. "You must enjoy realizing your ideal of a character so perfectly," she began.

"Yes? Did you feel that about it?" the actress returned. "It *is* a satisfaction. But if one has a strong conception of a part, I don't see how one can help rendering it strongly. And this Salome, she takes hold of me so powerfully. Her passion and her will, that won't stop at anything, seem to pierce through and through me. You can feel that she wouldn't mind killing a man or two to carry her point."

"That is certainly what *you* make one feel about her. And you make her very living, very actual."

"You are very good," said Mrs. Harley. "I am so glad you liked it. I was dreadfully afraid you wouldn't like it."

"Oh, I couldn't imagine your being afraid of anything," said

Louise, lightly. Her smile was one which the other woman might have known how to interpret rightly, but her husband alone among men could feel its peculiar quality. Godolphin beamed with apparent satisfaction in it.

"Wasn't Salome magnificent?" he said; and he magnanimously turned to the actress. "You will make everybody forget Haxard. You made *me* forget him."

"*I* didn't forget him though," said Mrs. Harley. "I was trying all the time to play up to him—and to Mrs. Maxwell."

The actor laughed his deep, mellow, hollow laugh, which was a fine work of art in itself, and said: "Mrs. Maxwell, you must let me present the other *dramatis personae* to you," and he introduced the whole cast of the play, one after another. Each said something of the Salome, how grand it was, how impassioned, how powerful. Maxwell stood by, listening, with his eyes on his wife's face, trying to read her thought.

They were silent most of the way home, and she only talked of indifferent things. When the door of their apartment shut them in with themselves alone, she broke out: "Horrible, horrible, horrible! Well, the play is ruined, ruined! We might as well die; or *I* might! I suppose *you* really liked it!"

Maxwell turned white with anger. "I didn't try to make her *think* I did, anyway. But I knew how you really felt, and I don't believe you deceived her very much, either. All the same I was ashamed to see you try."

"Don't talk to me—don't speak! She knew from every syllable I uttered that I perfectly loathed it, and I know that she tried to make it as hateful to me all the way through as she could. She played it *at* me, and she knew it *was* me. It was as if she kept saying all the time, 'How do you like my translation of your Boston girl into Alabama, or Mississippi, or Arkansas, or wherever I came from? This is the way you would have acted, if you were *me*!' Yes, that is the hideous part of it. Her nature has *come off* on the character, and I shall never see, or hear, or think, or dream Salome, after this, without having Yolande Havisham before me. She's spoiled the sweetest thing in my life. She's made me hate myself; she's made me hate *you*! Will you go out somewhere and get your lunch? I don't want anything myself, and just now I can't bear to look at you. Oh, you're not to blame, that I know of, if that's what you mean. Only go!"

"I can go out for lunch, certainly," said Maxwell "Perhaps you would rather I stayed out for dinner, too?"

"Don't be cruel, dearest. I am trying to control myself—"

"I shouldn't have thought it. You're not succeeding."

"No, not so well as you, if you hated this woman's Salome as much as I did. If it's always been as bad as it was to-day you've controlled yourself wonderfully well never to give me any hint of it, or prepare me for it in the least."

"How could I prepare you? You would have come to it with your own prepossessions, no matter what I said."

"Was that why you said nothing?"

"You would have hated it if she had played it with angelic perfection, because you hated her."

"Perhaps you think she really did play it with angelic perfection! Well, you needn't come back to dinner."

Louise passed into their room, to lay off her hat and sack.

"I will not come back at all, if you prefer," Maxwell called after her.

"I have no preferences in the matter," she mocked back.

XXIV

Maxwell and Louise had torn at each other's hearts till they were bleeding, and he wished to come back at once and she wished him to come, that they might hurt themselves still more savagely; but when this desire passed, they longed to meet and bind up one another's wounds. This better feeling brought them together before night-fall, when Maxwell returned, and Louise, at the sound of his latch-key in the door, ran to let him in.

"Mr. Godolphin is here," she said, in a loud, cheery voice, and he divined that he owed something of his eager welcome to her wish to keep him from resuming the quarrel unwittingly. "He has just come to talk over the rehearsal with you, and I wouldn't let him go. I was sure you would be back soon."

She put her finger to her lip, with whatever warning intention, and followed her husband into the presence of the actor, and almost into his arms, so rapturous was the meeting between them.

"Well," cried Godolphin, "I couldn't help looking in a moment to talk with you and Mrs. Maxwell about our Salome. I feel that she will make the fortune of the piece—of any piece. Doesn't Miss Havisham's rendition grow upon you? It's magnificent. It's on the grand scale. It's immense. The more I think about it, the more I'm impressed with it. She'll carry the house by storm. I've never seen anything like it; and I'm glad to find that Mrs. Maxwell feels just as I do about it." Maxwell looked at his wife, who returned his glance with a guiltless eye. "I was afraid she might feel the loss of things that certainly *are* lost in it. I don't say that Miss Havisham's Salome, superb as it is, is *your* Salome—or Mrs. Maxwell's. I've always fancied that Mrs. Maxwell had a great deal to do with that character, and—I don't know why—I've always thought of her when I've thought of *it*; but at the same time it's a splendid Salome. She makes it Southern, almost tropical. It isn't the Boston Salome. You may say that it is wanting in delicacy and the nice shades; but it's full of passion; there's nothing caviare to the general in it. The average audience will understand just what the girl that Miss Havisham gives is after, and she gives her so abundantly that there's no more doubt of the why than there is of the how. Sometimes I used to think the house couldn't follow Miss Pettrell in her subtle touches, but the house, to the topmost tier of the gallery, will get Miss Havisham's intention."

Godolphin was standing while he said all this, and Maxwell now asked: "Won't you sit down?"

The actor had his overcoat on his arm, and his hat in one hand. He tapped at his boot with the umbrella he held in the other. "No, I don't believe I will, thank you. The fact is, I just dropped in a moment to reassure you if you had misgivings about the Salome, and to give you my point of view."

Maxwell did not say anything; he looked at Louise again, and it seemed to her that he meant her to speak. She said, "Oh, we understood that we couldn't have all kinds of a Salome in one creation of the part; and I'm sure no one can

W. D. Howells

see Mrs. Harley in it without feeling her intensity."

"She's a force," said Godolphin. "And if, as we all decided," he continued, to Maxwell, "when we talked it over with Grayson, that a powerful Salome would heighten the effect of Haxard, she is going to make the success of the piece."

"*You* are going to make the success of the piece!" cried Louise.

"Ah, I sha'n't care if they forget me altogether," said the actor; "I shall forget myself." He laughed his mellow, hollow laugh, and gave his hand to Louise and then to Maxwell. "I'm so glad you feel as you do about it, and I don't wish you to lose your faith in our Salome for a moment. You've quite confirmed mine." He wrung the hands of each with a fervor of gratitude that left them with a disquiet which their eyes expressed to each other when he was gone.

"What does it mean?" asked Louise.

Maxwell shook his head. "It's beyond me."

"Brice," she appealed, after a moment, "do you think I had been saying anything to set him against her?"

"No," he returned, instantly. "Why should I suspect you of anything so base?"

Her throat was full, but she made out to say, "No, you are too generous, too good for such a thing;" and now she went on to eat humble-pie with a self-devotion which few women could practise. "I know that if I don't like having her I have no one but myself to thank for it. If I had never written to that miserable Mr. Sterne, or answered his advertisement, he would never have heard of your play, and nothing that has happened would have happened."

"No, you don't know that at all," said Maxwell; and it seemed to her that she must sink to her knees under his magnanimity. "The thing might have happened in a dozen different ways."

"No matter. I am to blame for it when it did happen; and now you will never hear another word from me. Would you like me to swear it?"

"That would be rather unpleasant," said Maxwell.

They both felt a great physical fatigue, and they neither had the wish to prolong the evening after dinner. Maxwell was going to lock the door of the apartment at nine o'clock, and then go to bed, when there came a ring at it. He opened it, and stood confronted with Grayson, looking very hot and excited.

"Can I come in a moment?" the manager asked. "Are you alone? Can I speak with you?"

"There's no one here but Mrs. Maxwell," said her husband, and he led the way into the parlor.

"And if you don't like," Louise confessed to have overheard him, "you needn't speak before her even."

"No, no," said the manager, "don't go! We may want your wisdom. We certainly want all the wisdom we can get on the question. It's about Godolphin."

"Godolphin?" they both echoed.

"Yes. He's given up the piece."

The manager drew out a letter, which he handed to Maxwell, and which Louise read with her husband, over his shoulder. It was addressed to Grayson, and began very formally.

"DEAR SIR:

"I wish to resign to you all claim I may have to a joint interest in Mr. Maxwell's piece, and to withdraw from the company formed for its representation. I feel that my part in it has been made secondary to another, and I have finally decided to relinquish it altogether. I trust that you will be able to supply my place, and I offer you my best wishes for the success of your enterprise.

"Yours very truly,
"L. GODOLPHIN."

The Maxwells did not look at each other; they both looked at the manager, and neither spoke.

"You see," said the manager, putting the letter back in its envelope, "it's Miss Havisham. I saw some signs of what was coming at the rehearsals, but I didn't think it would take such peremptory shape."

"Why, but he was here only a few hours ago, praising her to the skies," said Louise; and she hoped that she was keeping secret the guilty joy she felt; but probably it was not unknown to her husband.

"Oh, of course," said Grayson, with a laugh, "that was Godolphin's way. He may have felt all that he said; or he may have been trying to find out what Mr. Maxwell thought, and whether he could count upon him in a move against her."

"We said nothing," cried Louise, and she blessed heaven that she could truly say so, "which could possibly be distorted into that."

"I didn't suppose you had," said the manager. "But now we have got to act. We have got to do one of two things, and Godolphin knows it; we have got to let Miss Havisham go, or we have got to let him go. For my part I would much rather let him go. She is a finer artist every way, and she is more important to the success of the piece. But it would be more difficult to replace him than it would be to replace her, and he knows it. We could get Miss Pettrell at once for Salome, and we should have to look about for a Haxard. Still, I am disposed to drop Godolphin, if Mr. Maxwell feels as I do."

He looked at Maxwell; but Louise lowered her eyes, and would not influence her husband by so much as a glance. It seemed to her that he was a long time answering.

"I am satisfied with Godolphin's Haxard much better than I am with Miss Havisham's Salome, strong as it is. On the artistic side alone, I should prefer to keep Godolphin and let her go, if it could be done justly. Then, I know that Godolphin has made sacrifices and borne losses on account of the play, and I think that he has a right to a share in its success, if it has a chance of succeeding. He's jealous of Miss Havisham, of course; I could see that from the first minute; but he's earned the first place, and I'm not surprised he wants to keep it. I shouldn't like to lose it if I were he. I should say that we ought to make any concession he asks in that way."

"Very well," said Grayson. "He will ask to have our agreement with Mrs. Harley broken; and we can say that we were compelled to break it. I feel as you do, that he has some right on his side. She's a devilish provoking woman—excuse me, Mrs. Maxwell!—and I've seen her trying to take the centre

W. D. Howells

from Godolphin ever since the rehearsals began; but I don't like to be driven by him; still, there are worse things than being driven. In any case we have to accept the inevitable, and it's only a question of which inevitable we accept. Good-night. I will see Godolphin at once. Good-night, Mrs. Maxwell. We shall expect you to do what you can in consoling your fair neighbor and reconciling *her* to the inevitable." Louise did not know whether this was ironical or not, and she did not at all like the laugh from Maxwell which greeted the suggestion.

"*I* shall have to reconcile Sterne, and I don't believe that will be half so easy."

The manager's words were gloomy, but there was an imaginable relief in his tone and a final cheerfulness in his manner. He left the Maxwells to a certain embarrassment in each other's presence. Louise was the first to break the silence that weighed upon them both.

"Brice, did you decide that way to please me?"

"I am not such a fool," said Maxwell.

"Because," she said, "if you did, you did very wrong, and I don't believe any good could come of it."

Yet she did not seem altogether averse to the risks involved; and in fact she could not justly accuse herself of what had happened, however devoutly she had wished for such a consummation.

XXV

It was Miss Havisham and not Godolphin who appeared to
the public as having ended the combination their managers
had formed. The interviewing on both sides continued until
the interest of the quarrel was lost in that of the first
presentation of the play, when the impression that Miss
Havisham had been ill-used was effaced by the impression
made by Miss Pettrell in the part of Salome. Her performance was not only successful in the delicacy and refinement which her friends expected of her, but she brought to
the work a vivid yet purely feminine force which took them
by surprise and made the public her own. No one in the
house could have felt, as the Maxwells felt, a certain quality
in it which it would be extremely difficult to characterize
without overstating it. Perhaps Louise felt this more even
than her husband, for when she appealed to him, he would
scarcely confess to a sense of it; but from time to time in the
stronger passages she was aware of an echo, to the ear and to
the eye, of a more passionate personality than Miss Pettrell's.
Had Godolphin profited by his knowledge of Miss
Havisham's creation, and had he imparted to Miss Pettrell,
who never saw it, hints of it which she used in her own
creation of the part? If he had, just what was the measure and
the nature of his sin? Louise tormented herself with this
question, while a sense of the fact went as often as it came,
and left her in a final doubt of it. What was certain was that

if Godolphin had really committed this crime, of which he might have been quite unconsciously guilty, Miss Pettrell was wholly innocent of it; and, indeed, the effect she made might very well have been imagined by herself, and only have borne this teasing resemblance by pure accident. Godolphin was justly punished if he were culpable, and he suffered an eclipse in any case which could not have been greater from Miss Havisham. There were recalls for the chief actors at every fall of the curtain, and at the end of the third act, in which Godolphin had really been magnificent, there began to be cries of "Author! Author!" and a messenger appeared in the box where the Maxwells sat and begged the author, in Godolphin's name, to come behind at once. The next thing that Louise knew the actor was leading her husband on the stage and they were both bowing to the house, which shouted at them and had them back once and twice and still shouted, but now with a certain confusion of voices in its demand, which continued till the author came on a fourth time, led by the actor as before, and himself leading the heroine of his piece. Then the storm of applause left no doubt that the will of the house had been rightly interpreted.

Louise sat still, with the tears blurring the sight before her. They were not only proud and happy tears, but they were tears of humble gratitude that it was Miss Pettrell, and not Mrs. Harley, whom her husband was leading on to share his triumph. She did not think her own desert was great; but she could not tax herself with any wrong that she had not at least tried to repair; she felt that what she had escaped she could not have suffered, and that Heaven was merciful to her weakness, if not just to her merit. Perhaps this was why she was so humble and so grateful.

There arose in her a vague fear as to what Godolphin might do in the case of a Salome who was certainly no more subordinated to his Haxard than Miss Havisham's, or what new demands he might not make upon the author; but Maxwell came back to her with a message from the actor, which he wished conveyed with his congratulations upon the success of the piece. This was to tell her of his engagement to Miss Pettrell, which had suddenly taken place that day, and which he thought there could be no moment so fit to impart to her as that of their common triumph.

Louise herself went behind at the end of the piece, and made herself acceptable to both the artists in her cordial good wishes. Neither of them resented the arch intention with which she said to Godolphin, "I suppose you won't mind such a beautiful Salome as Miss Pettrell has given us, now that it's to be all in the family."

Miss Pettrell answered for him with as complete an intelligence: "Oh, I shall know how to subdue her to his Haxard, if she ever threatens the peace of the domestic hearth."

That Salome has never done so in any serious measure Maxwell argues from the fact that, though the Godolphins have now been playing his piece together for a whole year since their marriage, they have not yet been divorced.

THE END

W. D. Howells

ABOUT THE AUTHOR

William Dean Howells (March 1, 1837 – May 11, 1920) was an American realist author and literary critic.

Born in Martins Ferry, Ohio, originally Martinsville, to William Cooper and Mary Dean Howells, Howells was the second of eight children. His father was a newspaper editor and printer, and the father moved frequently around Ohio. Howells began to help his father with typesetting and printing work at an early age. In 1852, his father arranged to have one of Howells' poems published in the Ohio State Journal without telling him.

He wrote his first novel, The Wedding Journey, in 1872, but his literary reputation took off with the realist novel, A Modern Instance, published in 1882, which described the decay of a marriage. His 1885 novel The Rise of Silas Lapham is perhaps his best known, describing the rise and fall of an American entrepreneur in the paint business. His social views were also strongly reflected in the novels Annie Kilburn (1888) and A Hazard of New Fortunes (1890). He was particularly outraged by the trials resulting from the Haymarket Riot.

In 1904, he was one of the first seven chosen for membership in the American Academy of Arts and Letters, of which he became president.

Choose from Thousands of 1stWorldLibrary Classics By

A. M. Barnard
Ada Leverson
Adolphus William Ward
Aesop
Agatha Christie
Alexander Aaronsohn
Alexander Kielland
Alexandre Dumas
Alfred Gatty
Alfred Ollivant
Alice Duer Miller
Alice Turner Curtis
Alice Dunbar
Allen Chapman
Alleyne Ireland
Ambrose Bierce
Amelia E. Barr
Amory H. Bradford
Andrew Lang
Andrew McFarland Davis
Andy Adams
Angela Brazil
Anna Alice Chapin
Anna Sewell
Annie Besant
Annie Hamilton Donnell
Annie Payson Call
Annie Roe Carr
Annonaymous
Anton Chekhov
Archibald Lee Fletcher
Arnold Bennett
Arthur C. Benson
Arthur Conan Doyle
Arthur M. Winfield
Arthur Ransome
Arthur Schnitzler
Arthur Train
Atticus
B.H. Baden-Powell
B. M. Bower
B. C. Chatterjee
Baroness Emmuska Orczy
Baroness Orczy
Basil King
Bayard Taylor
Ben Macomber
Bertha Muzzy Bower
Bjornstjerne Bjornson

Booth Tarkington
Boyd Cable
Bram Stoker
C. Collodi
C. E. Orr
C. M. Ingleby
Carolyn Wells
Catherine Parr Traill
Charles A. Eastman
Charles Amory Beach
Charles Dickens
Charles Dudley Warner
Charles Farrar Browne
Charles Ives
Charles Kingsley
Charles Klein
Charles Hanson Towne
Charles Lathrop Pack
Charles Romyn Dake
Charles Whibley
Charles Willing Beale
Charlotte M. Braeme
Charlotte M. Yonge
Charlotte Perkins Stetson
Clair W. Hayes
Clarence Day Jr.
Clarence E. Mulford
Clemence Housman
Confucius
Coningsby Dawson
Cornelis DeWitt Wilcox
Cyril Burleigh
D. H. Lawrence
Daniel Defoe
David Garnett
Dinah Craik
Don Carlos Janes
Donald Keyhoe
Dorothy Kilner
Dougan Clark
Douglas Fairbanks
E. Nesbit
E. P. Roe
E. Phillips Oppenheim
E. S. Brooks
Earl Barnes
Edgar Rice Burroughs
Edith Van Dyne
Edith Wharton

Edward Everett Hale
Edward J. O'Biren
Edward S. Ellis
Edwin L. Arnold
Eleanor Atkins
Eleanor Hallowell Abbott
Eliot Gregory
Elizabeth Gaskell
Elizabeth McCracken
Elizabeth Von Arnim
Ellem Key
Emerson Hough
Emilie F. Carlen
Emily Bronte
Emily Dickinson
Enid Bagnold
Enilor Macartney Lane
Erasmus W. Jones
Ernie Howard Pie
Ethel May Dell
Ethel Turner
Ethel Watts Mumford
Eugene Sue
Eugenie Foa
Eugene Wood
Eustace Hale Ball
Evelyn Everett-green
Everard Cotes
F. H. Cheley
F. J. Cross
F. Marion Crawford
Fannie E. Newberry
Federick Austin Ogg
Ferdinand Ossendowski
Fergus Hume
Florence A. Kilpatrick
Fremont B. Deering
Francis Bacon
Francis Darwin
Frances Hodgson Burnett
Frances Parkinson Keyes
Frank Gee Patchin
Frank Harris
Frank Jewett Mather
Frank L. Packard
Frank V. Webster
Frederic Stewart Isham
Frederick Trevor Hill
Frederick Winslow Taylor

Friedrich Kerst
Friedrich Nietzsche
Fyodor Dostoyevsky
G.A. Henty
G.K. Chesterton
Gabrielle E. Jackson
Garrett P. Serviss
Gaston Leroux
George A. Warren
George Ade
Geroge Bernard Shaw
George Cary Eggleston
George Durston
George Ebers
George Eliot
George Gissing
George MacDonald
George Meredith
George Orwell
George Sylvester Viereck
George Tucker
George W. Cable
George Wharton James
Gertrude Atherton
Gordon Casserly
Grace E. King
Grace Gallatin
Grace Greenwood
Grant Allen
Guillermo A. Sherwell
Gulielma Zollinger
Gustav Flaubert
H. A. Cody
H. B. Irving
H.C. Bailey
H. G. Wells
H. H. Munro
H. Irving Hancock
H. R. Naylor
H. Rider Haggard
H. W. C. Davis
Haldeman Julius
Hall Caine
Hamilton Wright Mabie
Hans Christian Andersen
Harold Avery
Harold McGrath
Harriet Beecher Stowe
Harry Castlemon
Harry Coghill
Harry Houidini

Hayden Carruth
Helent Hunt Jackson
Helen Nicolay
Hendrik Conscience
Hendy David Thoreau
Henri Barbusse
Henrik Ibsen
Henry Adams
Henry Ford
Henry Frost
Henry James
Henry Jones Ford
Henry Seton Merriman
Henry W Longfellow
Herbert A. Giles
Herbert Carter
Herbert N. Casson
Herman Hesse
Hildegard G. Frey
Homer
Honore De Balzac
Horace B. Day
Horace Walpole
Horatio Alger Jr.
Howard Pyle
Howard R. Garis
Hugh Lofting
Hugh Walpole
Humphry Ward
Ian Maclaren
Inez Haynes Gillmore
Irving Bacheller
Isabel Cecilia Williams
Isabel Hornibrook
Israel Abrahams
Ivan Turgenev
J.G.Austin
J. Henri Fabre
J. M. Barrie
J. M. Walsh
J. Macdonald Oxley
J. R. Miller
J. S. Fletcher
J. S. Knowles
J. Storer Clouston
J. W. Duffield
Jack London
Jacob Abbott
James Allen
James Andrews
James Baldwin

James Branch Cabell
James DeMille
James Joyce
James Lane Allen
James Lane Allen
James Oliver Curwood
James Oppenheim
James Otis
James R. Driscoll
Jane Abbott
Jane Austen
Jane L. Stewart
Janet Aldridge
Jens Peter Jacobsen
Jerome K. Jerome
Jessie Graham Flower
John Buchan
John Burroughs
John Cournos
John F. Kennedy
John Gay
John Glasworthy
John Habberton
John Joy Bell
John Kendrick Bangs
John Milton
John Philip Sousa
John Taintor Foote
Jonas Lauritz Idemil Lie
Jonathan Swift
Joseph A. Altsheler
Joseph Carey
Joseph Conrad
Joseph E. Badger Jr
Joseph Hergesheimer
Joseph Jacobs
Jules Vernes
Julian Hawthrone
Julie A Lippmann
Justin Huntly McCarthy
Kakuzo Okakura
Karle Wilson Baker
Kate Chopin
Kenneth Grahame
Kenneth McGaffey
Kate Langley Bosher
Kate Langley Bosher
Katherine Cecil Thurston
Katherine Stokes
L. A. Abbot
L. T. Meade

L. Frank Baum
Latta Griswold
Laura Dent Crane
Laura Lee Hope
Laurence Housman
Lawrence Beasley
Leo Tolstoy
Leonid Andreyev
Lewis Carroll
Lewis Sperry Chafer
Lilian Bell
Lloyd Osbourne
Louis Hughes
Louis Joseph Vance
Louis Tracy
Louisa May Alcott
Lucy Fitch Perkins
Lucy Maud Montgomery
Luther Benson
Lydia Miller Middleton
Lyndon Orr
M. Corvus
M. H. Adams
Margaret E. Sangster
Margret Howth
Margaret Vandercook
Margaret W. Hungerford
Margret Penrose
Maria Edgeworth
Maria Thompson Daviess
Mariano Azuela
Marion Polk Angellotti
Mark Overton
Mark Twain
Mary Austin
Mary Catherine Crowley
Mary Cole
Mary Hastings Bradley
Mary Roberts Rinehart
Mary Rowlandson
M. Wollstonecraft Shelley
Maud Lindsay
Max Beerbohm
Myra Kelly
Nathaniel Hawthrone
Nicolo Machiavelli
O. F. Walton
Oscar Wilde

Owen Johnson
P.G. Wodehouse
Paul and Mabel Thorne
Paul G. Tomlinson
Paul Severing
Percy Brebner
Percy Keese Fitzhugh
Peter B. Kyne
Plato
Quincy Allen
R. Derby Holmes
R. L. Stevenson
R. S. Ball
Rabindranath Tagore
Rahul Alvares
Ralph Bonehill
Ralph Henry Barbour
Ralph Victor
Ralph Waldo Emmerson
Rene Descartes
Ray Cummings
Rex Beach
Rex E. Beach
Richard Harding Davis
Richard Jefferies
Richard Le Gallienne
Robert Barr
Robert Frost
Robert Gordon Anderson
Robert L. Drake
Robert Lansing
Robert Lynd
Robert Michael Ballantyne
Robert W. Chambers
Rosa Nouchette Carey
Rudyard Kipling
Saint Augustine
Samuel B. Allison
Samuel Hopkins Adams
Sarah Bernhardt
Sarah C. Hallowell
Selma Lagerlof
Sherwood Anderson
Sigmund Freud
Standish O'Grady
Stanley Weyman
Stella Benson
Stella M. Francis

Stephen Crane
Stewart Edward White
Stijn Streuvels
Swami Abhedananda
Swami Parmananda
T. S. Ackland
T. S. Arthur
The Princess Der Ling
Thomas A. Janvier
Thomas A Kempis
Thomas Anderton
Thomas Bailey Aldrich
Thomas Bulfinch
Thomas De Quincey
Thomas Dixon
Thomas H. Huxley
Thomas Hardy
Thomas More
Thornton W. Burgess
U. S. Grant
Upton Sinclair
Valentine Williams
Various Authors
Vaughan Kester
Victor Appleton
Victor G. Durham
Victoria Cross
Virginia Woolf
Wadsworth Camp
Walter Camp
Walter Scott
Washington Irving
Wilbur Lawton
Wilkie Collins
Willa Cather
Willard F. Baker
William Dean Howells
William le Queux
W. Makepeace Thackeray
William W. Walter
William Shakespeare
Winston Churchill
Yei Theodora Ozaki
Yogi Ramacharaka
Young E. Allison
Zane Grey